I0683372

The Afterlife Mortals

By

A.M. Romero

AARON
PUBLISHING

Copyright © 2018 by Aaron Publishing

www.aaronpublishing.com

All rights reserved. No part of this publication may be reproduced, stored in a retrieval system, or transmitted, in any form or by any other means—electronic, mechanical, photocopying, recording, or otherwise—without prior written permission of Aaron Publishing.

Printed in the United States of America

First Printing, March 2018

ISBN 978-0-9989385-3-0

Published by

Aaron Publishing

PO Box 1144

Shelbyville, TN 37162

www.aaronpublishing.com

To God always and forevermore.
To family that I adore and friends that I cherish.
This one's for you.

Chapter I

Pancakes with a Side Order of Writer's Block

Jo Silver knew the minute she woke up this was another day for her writer's block to continue its long haul of emptiness.

She had spent most of the night scribbling and doodling, trying to find a good storyline for her characters that had only names from Google and partial descriptions of their appearance, only to be still stuck on the seventh day of her Writer's Block dilemma.

She had no idea there was actually a word describing a writer who is stuck on his or her story and can't brainstorm anything, but there was and she hated it. Writer's Block is probably -- from what she read on the internet -- the most common struggle that all writers get at some point in their writing life.

"'Write a book,' they say," Jo muttered under her covers. "'It should be easy for you.' they say." Jo had never "really" been interested in writing a book at first. Her teachers were just amazed at how good she was at capturing their attention with her words in essays and English projects. She didn't know how, but she was just good at writing...really good actually. It was her best friend Avy who suggested that she should write a book.

"Just try it and see," her best friend told her. "If you don't think it's your thing, then at least you'll know. Give it an effort and who knows? Maybe I'm best friends with a best-selling author."

So Jo tried it. She started off with about four main characters—Ozias, Dezmon, E.J., and Abaddon -- who were all best friends living in a dystopian world -- that was still in need of work. She thought she had a pretty good idea of what it was going to be about but when she got to writing the actual chapters, nothing came to mind on how to get from Point A to Point B. So that was when her Writer's Block happened.

Jo then decided to change the setting of the book. She went from outer space (always confused during science class) to medieval times (but those names wouldn't have seemed accurate there and it was hard enough finding them in the first place) ending up in a more realistic setting (let's face it, she's living realistically). But what would these four do in this plain, dull world? There was no way that they could solve the crime because she wouldn't know how to make the story mysterious like in the Nancy Drew series. She thought of time travel, but then again, she would have to figure out the setting and the time period they would land in, not to mention learning how to make it accurate. There was no way she could write a romance book! Jo herself has never had a boyfriend. How could she ever describe any romantic relationship with these guys pairing up with girls? If that were to happen, then she would have to create four girls which would add more characters leading to confusion and whatnot. They're boys, for crying out loud! So what do boys do that makes a story interesting?

Her teachers had told her when she asked for advice to just go out and be active then maybe an idea would come to mind. She tried writing prompts she found on Pinterest but nothing seemed to click for her story.

Jo was just stuck with only a white empty document on her laptop screen.

"Pancakes!" hollered her mom from downstairs. Sleepily, she got up and went to her closet to get clothes -- and the black bandana she always wore around her left wrist -- then disappeared into the bathroom. Within ten minutes, Jo went down the hall with the backpack she was taking to school and was welcomed by the smell of vanilla cinnamon pancakes as she sat at the kitchen table.

"Morning, Jo," her mother said, placing pancakes on the plate in front of her. Looking at Jo's face, she immediately knew the cause of her daughter's drowsiness. "Still on Writer's Block?"

"Maybe writing's not my thing," Jo said, taking a bite of her delicious pancakes.

"Honey, it just takes time," her father said, coming in ready to go to work. "Maybe the idea is already inside of you and all you have to do is wait for it to be revealed."

"Your father's right," her mother chimed in, "Ideas come when they think the time's right."

"I guess," she said, looking at the stove's digital clock. "Crap! I'm late!" Jo devoured the rest of her pancakes in a flash and after kissing both her parent's goodbye, she raced out the door, heading towards the bus stop.

Luckily, she made it before the last few kids -- including Avy who was stalling the bus driver for her -- got on the bus. "You're late," Avy told her as they both got on together. Avy's blonde hair was in a tight, slick bun at the crown of her head. She wore a blouse and thin scarf with a skirt and leggings underneath. Covering her feet were her soft boots she wore all the time. If you didn't know she did ballet, you probably would know just by looking at her. Comparing the two, Avy dressed like a casual ballerina, and Jo dressed almost like a rocker chic from the sixties.

"Way to state the obvious!" Jo huffed as they got their seats right before the bus moved again. Jo had on the usual -- which she always wore -- a t-shirt that was tucked in her high-waist shorts and her thin legs covered by tights that only went up to her ankles. Her brunette hair was either loose or in a ponytail and she always wore a leather jacket over most outfits and of course, her red converse everywhere she went.

"I seriously thought you called in sick without even telling me," her best friend admitted. "I mean, I seriously didn't think you would be this late to the bus stop so I came up with like over a hundred scenarios of what happened to you. One of them was getting killed by a "sharknado." With as much stupidity as there was in all of the Sharknado movies, Avy and Jo still found themselves laughing every time they watched them. It was too dumb and funny to hate them and it was one of the things they did for fun together.

"Well, I'm sorry that it's been a week of nothing going on up here," Jo replied pointing at her temple.

"Still on that Writer's Block?" Avy asked. "No wonder you look like a walker. You put too much blush on."

"You know I don't wear makeup," Jo told her.

"I was just making sure you weren't a full-on zombie yet," Avy teased, checking her own makeup in her tiny mirror she held in her hands.

"I'm still awake so you can't put any foundation on me if that's what you're thinking."

"Oh darn!" Avy said, snapping her fingers. "Looks like you're partially yourself."

The bus driver dropped them off in front of Shaw High School about thirty minutes before the school bell would ring for class. As Jo and Avy got off, they made their way into the school building until Jo's eye caught something in the school parking lot -- or she thought she did.

"What's up?" Avy asked her.

"I thought I saw something weird."

"Oh-kay?" Avy asked. "Whatever it is, I'm sure it's not something like -- oh I don't know -- a crank."

Jo looked at her, "Seriously, a crank as in The Maze Runner Cranks?"

"I mean it's not like we both read the book and watched the movie or anything."

"C'mon then," Jo said, pulling her brunette hair back behind her. "Let's get to class before the Peacekeepers find us."

***

Jo was so anxious for her lunch period throughout all her morning classes. She somehow couldn't concentrate on the lesson because all she could think about was how to get out of her Writer's Block. It was crowding her focus at school that she barely understood most of the things they taught in her classes. When lunch came around, Jo told herself that she had to let the story go in order to focus on getting a good grade. Even though she mentally decided it, Avy could see it on Jo's face.

"You're quitting the book writing thing, aren't ya?"

"What---?"

"Don't even, Josephine Silver---."

"Hey!" Jo exclaimed, covering Avy's mouth. "Don't say the full name in public!"

"I will if you don't admit that I'm right," Avy threatened with a smirk.

"Fine," Jo grumbled, removing her hand from Avy's mouth. "You're right, I'm giving it up."

"You haven't even started the first chapter."

"That's the problem. I haven't started the first chapter because I don't even know what to write about. I mean it's easier to write essays and school lit papers, but an *entire* story? I don't think it's my thing."

"Well," Avy started, "What if it is and you're going to give up on it right now?"

"Avy, c'mon," Jo told her. "It's not."

"Jo Silver! A best-selling author of many books that turned into blockbuster movies and TV shows," she said, sounding like a news reporter. "Oh wait, she quit before all that had even happened."

"Shut up!" Jo said, shoving her best friend playfully.

"Don't be like Emma Swan who for so long had denied the fact that she was the savior," Avy told her.

"Okay, okay, I'll give it a try."

"Thatta girl!" Avy exclaimed happily. "Oh and you can't forget! Ballet Recital is this Friday at six. I'll get there around four if you wanna join me."

"Hmmm, let me think about it," Jo replied, "Okay, I'll go."

After awhile of discussing the facts, clues, and unsolved mysteries of their all-time favorite TV show *Once Upon A Time*, Avy had taken Jo's offer of getting her a Coke from the vending machine before their lunch period ended. Jo's mind was still searching for a story as she walked towards the vending machine.

What if, she asked, staring at the Cokes that were in front of her. *There was an extinction of soda? That's stupid, Jo. Why in the world would you think of that?*

She placed the dollars inside the machine and pressed the buttons leading to the Cokes.

Monsters taking over what was left of Mars? That's a children's book for sure!

One of the Cokes got stuck during the process of delivery. In frustration, Jo banged her hands hard enough to attempt to get it unstuck but didn't succeed. "Stupid machine! Why won't you work?" When she finally stopped banging it, she noticed something on the machine's glass display of sodas. There was a reflection of someone that -- from what she could tell -- had blonde hair and was wearing all white with the face of worry. Then there came a petrified cry from some random girl in the school that led into multiple screams and footsteps running. When she turned around to find the owner of the reflection, no one was there behind her but a boy taller than her wearing all black with a handgun pointed right at her.

Jo dropped her change in fright as she raised her hands to where he could see them, not even worrying about what was happening around her. She kept her eyes on the gun that was trembling in his hands, making the clicking sound that meant it was loaded. His eyes had dark circles underneath, indicating he could be exhausted at this point. He had dark hair, not-too-pale skin, a t-shirt, jeans, and a dark zip up jacket with the hood over his head. Jo looked at his face for the longest time, even though it was hard to see his whole face in his hood.

"What do you want?" Jo managed to choke out.

"I don't want to do this," he said to her. Once she heard his voice, she knew he wasn't a complete stranger. She knew him from somewhere but it wasn't from school. For some reason, it was hard to picture where she knew him from. It felt like years of thinking until she noticed something that made her brain click in realization. There was a black bandana that was wrapped around his wrist -- the same color and wrist Jo had always put *her* bandana on.

"Axel?" she asked, knowing that she only knew one Axel Lardica in all of her life.

"I'm sorry Jo," Axel said with a cracked voice. "I'm so sorry, Jo. But if I'm starting over, I'm doing it with you."

Jo Silver fell back from the impact of the bullet that went straight to her heart and lost sight of everything she had ahead of her.

Chapter II

Dead as a Ghost

Josephine Silver was running as fast she could down her street when she realized she was being chased by that older group of boys again—heart beating fast, legs already burning within, breath hard to catch. This had happened multiple times since she moved into the military town only a few months ago. This same group of boys was the reason why she hated the move. Once she hit her new school, they found her as their new bait and have hunted her ever since.

Cutting through the backyards of her neighborhood, she knew she was running out of energy. But she had to keep running, for if she stopped it would happen again. The torture would come again. But her legs couldn't take it any longer so they forced her to stop and catch her breath. She could hear their voices coming closer as she bent over to catch her breath, hands on her knees. She couldn't outrun them and she knew it. Josephine knew that however far she ran, they would always be just yards right behind her. She was tired of running. Yeah, she was only six years old, being chased by tough, mean eight-year-old boys, but she just wanted to belong somewhere and not be hunted down by......

Something took hold of her arm and jerked her inside a fenced in yard. Her back had been gently but firmly guided against the fence wall as a boy her age kept a hand on her shoulder. He had dark hair with such blue eyes, you couldn't attempt to ignore them. He put a finger on his mouth indicating she had to be quiet. She nodded as he quickly closed the back gate. The boys that were chasing her ran beside the fence line and past the gate. Josephine barely heard their voices anymore after a good few minutes.

"You okay?" The boy asked her.

"Yeah, thanks," she said to him. Then, "I'm Josephine Silver."

"Axel Lardica," he said, "A-X-E-L, not L-E. My dad wanted to find a way to make it look different."

"Oh," Josephine said, sounding interested. "That's cool."

"Can I call you Jo?" the boy asked. "I don't think 'Josephine' will come out completely when I holler your name."

"'Jo' sounds cool!" She said excitedly in a soft tone. "I like it. 'Jo Silver.'"

"It suits you," Axel told her. "Those boys always find a way to mess with someone."

"Yeah," she agreed.

"Wanna know how to fight back?"

"You wanna help me?" Jo asked.

"Yeah," Axel replied, "You can trust me. I got your back no matter what."

***

Jo opened her eyes after hearing another gunshot echo in her ears. Everything was foggy in her sight as she tried to concentrate on making her head stop throbbing. She had no idea what was really going on until her vision had cleared up. In her view, it looked like her school ceiling from where she lay. Sitting up with her head still spinning, she saw Avy running up towards her, going through the sea of teenagers that were running in the opposite direction during the process.

"Avy! It's okay! I'm okay......!" Jo called but stopped when she realized Avy ran past her as if she wasn't there. She didn't understand it until she turned and saw Avy kneeling at a body where a pool of blood was flowing from the chest. Getting up as her throbbing was somewhat fading, Jo looked over Avy's shoulder and saw that it wasn't just somebody lying there, it was *her*. It was the same loose brunette hair, the same green eyes, the same pair of high waist shorts with leggings and shirt, the same pair of red converse -- everything was all same. Why was she standing here and yet dead on the floor over there?

This can't be real. Jo kept thinking, *This is just some nightmare. Some kind of crazy dream.*

Avy sat there, sobbing so hard for her best friend, calling Jo's name as teachers were already calling 911 and making sure the rest of the students were safely out of the building. One teacher tried to get Avy outside, but she wouldn't budge. She wouldn't let Jo's body go.

Jo knelt beside her. "Avy, I'm okay! I'm here!" She put her hand out to touch her shoulder, but it went right through Avy as if she were now smoke or mist or-or even a ghost.

Jo Silver was really *dead!*

Dead as a ghost!

She couldn't be. This is too impossible for it to be real.

Avy was eventually taken away from the Jo's body that lay on the school cafeteria's floor by one of the art teachers when everyone scattered outside and headed toward the field. It was hard to pry Avy out of her misery but she eventually joined everyone outside, leaving Jo on the floor, alone in the cafeteria.

"Jo, *wake up!* Get up! You're in a bad dream!" Jo screamed. "This isn't real! I'm not dead! I can't be dead!" She tried everything, pinching, banging her head— that was already hurting, slapping herself. It didn't work. None of it did. With her knees on the ground, she bent her body down, legs against her chest and hands on her head. "This can't be real! It's not real! I'm not dead! I can't be dead!" Her voice echoed from the floor. No one would help because she couldn't be heard from where she was; it was as if she was never there. Was this what it's like to really feel invisible, to not only be invisible but to watch the aftermath of finding yourself on the floor, draining out your own blood? Was this really what it's like to disappear from existence? To die?

No, it couldn't be. It felt too much like a dream she couldn't control. This had to be some dream she hadn't woke up from yet.

Jo sat up—her face stained with tears, as she looked around her. She was startled when she found out that she wasn't the only dead body there was at the school. On the floor as well with a bullet hole through the side of his head was the one and only Axel Lardica. His thick blood had already soaked his black bandana that was around his left wrist -- the same wrist Jo put her bandana on. His last expression froze on his face was of fear as if he was afraid of something he saw. The gun was beside his dead body, so Jo figured he must've killed himself after he'd shot her.

This has to be some kind of crazy dream for Axel to really be in it. Jo thought to herself.

What had happened to the Axel she knew? The Axel she knew would never do something like this, which is why Jo wondered if this really was a dream. He had the same face as him, the same dark hair, the same not-so-pale-skin, but was older than the last time she had seen him. If this really was the Axel she knew that had been absent from her life since fifth grade, why was he a school shooter in her dream?

I'm so sorry, Jo. But if I'm starting over, I'm doing it with you. His voice had echoed that sentence in her head for quite some time, making her wonder why she was his motive to be a school shooter? Why *Axel?* Why -- out of all people -- did Axel play the role of the shooter? And what could he possibly mean about starting over? He told her when they were kids he wouldn't let anything happen to her. But here -- in this dream -- he had shot her.

Jo realized something...if she was dead and she was a ghost, wouldn't he be too? If so, where was he?

***

"Don't worry Avy, it's going to be okay," she told her best friend -- who had left the building moments ago -- knowing that she probably wouldn't be able to hear her. She got up and started to walk around the school looking for the killer. He had to be somewhere. Maybe in order to wake up from this nightmare, Jo had to find the shooter.

As she searched down the school hallways, she went through all the other teenagers and teachers who were all bolting from the classrooms and through the main doors. Jo saw fear in all the faces that passed by her; screams from some trying to get away from the cafeteria as fast as possible. It was like when the random crowd runs away from some kind of alien, or dinosaurs, or even a giant wave crashing into a building. But they were all running from just a kid with a gun who was already dead. But most of them didn't know that. Not one of them stopped to look at her. It felt odd. Of course, she and Avy weren't popular at school but they were known in some way. Sometimes as "those two girls", other times as "the odd friends." So in a way, they were invisible, but Jo had never realized that being really invisible and being mentally invisible are two different things.

"Jo," came a voice from behind her. In a flash, Jo turned around only to find the other side of the empty hallway. She thought she heard a voice right behind her. Was she losing it?

"Josephine," the voice echoed. She turned back to the direction she was heading only to find herself still alone in the hallway.

"Who's there?" she replied. "Axel?"

"Fear not," the voice told her, still echoing either in her head or in the hallway. It sounded like a boy's voice that could've been around her age or older. But it definitely wasn't Axel, or was she wrong?

"I'm not scared of you," she stated, balling up her hands into a fist, wondering how long until she would eventually wake up for school on Monday. She turned around in a full circle, trying to find out where the voice was coming from.

"It's not me you should be scared of," the voice told her, still not showing himself to her. Just when things couldn't get weirder, a loud cry boomed through the hallways followed by an evil laugh that ran chills through Jo's spine. The cry sounded like it was in danger and she knew it. That evil laugh wasn't some person messing around. Something was wrong with him.

Without thinking, Jo ran towards the screeching cry of help that was Axel Lardica himself.

Chapter III

Ozias and Dezmon

The terrible sounds of help and what sounded like torture led Jo to the open double doors of the school's auditorium. Quietly, she pressed her body against the wall right behind one of the double doors trying to look at what was going on in the auditorium through the crack between the door and the door frame. But what she saw was something that was beyond the category of insane.

On the auditorium stage was Axel -- wearing the same thing he "died" in -- on the ground in fear with black chains cuffed around his hands and neck as he tried to shove himself away from the dark figure that held the other end of his chains. The figure looked about the same height as both Jo and Axel and it had seemed odd that it was Axel who was pleading for mercy until you really took a good look at his opponent. Shadowing over him was a boy that seemed to be around their age wearing all black clothes that matched his own coal hair. He had pale skin but it looked to be covered up by something dark that had stained his entire body -- as if where he came from was filled with this dark dust that was on him. He revealed a demonic expression on his face as he yanked Axel closer by the chains, making Axel's face meet the dark boy's. When Jo squinted her eyes to focus on the vision, she panicked when she saw that the dark boy had enormous, pure black wings. What was even stranger was that this dark boy looked terribly familiar.

"I've been waiting for this moment for a long time," the dark figure told Axel. Then without any warning, he let out a horrifying, screechy cry at Axel's face. He sounded and almost seemed like a boy beast. "Why are you so scared? You should be happy that you're here. After all, that's the whole reason why you did what you did, right? So you could start over, right?"

This was some dream. If Jo could just get out of her hiding spot and take off without ever looking back at this vision -- this nightmare part of the dream -- but either her legs wouldn't let her ignore this or this was a part of the dream she couldn't move away from. Watching this winged kid mocking Axel made her go back to the time she was in that same position with the group of boys ganging up on her -- and Axel was there to help her.

It was pretty obvious what she had to do next. Tiptoeing out from her hiding spot, she went around the corner to find the pair of double doors leading right to the stage. She tried to grab the handle but her hand went through it like a hologram.

Crap! She still was in ghost form. Jo tried again but it still went through. Before becoming frustrated, the situation gave her an idea. Taking a deep breath, she charged at the door and ended up on the other side, facing the stage in front of her. The beast kid's back -- along with his enormous wings -- were facing her as she tried to think of what to do next. He was still toying with Axel by pulling and tugging on the chain. Watching the boy do this along with Jo's memory of Axel boiled up anger inside of her.

At full speed, she raced towards the two and jumped on the dark beast kid, taking hold of his coal wings with both hands. The demonic beast screeched again making Jo's ears hurt as he stumbled backward, releasing the chains attached to Axel from his dark hands. Flapping his wings ferociously, Jo still held on until he reached back with his hands and took hold of her wrists. He flung her over to where she was now in front of him.

Jo did her best not to look down as the demonic beast brought her face closer to his by gripping her shirt with his dark-stained hands. Looking at his face, she was more in shock than scared of the dark figure that basically was watching her fear come to life in this awful, awful dream.

"Josephine Silver," he spat at her, "How are you doing up here? Wait, remind me again— are you scared of heights?"

"Who are you?" she asked, ignoring his sarcasm.

"Funny that you didn't ask how I knew your name, but who cares, right? All these mortals want to know who *I* am. But I think you're the only mortal that knows *exactly* who I am."

"How exactly?" she asked, trying not to sound scared.

"Let me answer your first question first," he told her, "They call me Dezmon. And do you wanna know what I do for a living?"

Jo didn't reply because she couldn't believe this was actually Dezmon -- one of the four characters she had created in her unknown story. His entire figure -- besides the dark clothes and wings -- was exactly how she had pictured him in her head. It was a crazy thing to see Jo's character right in front of her! Dezmon didn't wait for her to answer -- until he got interrupted.

"You're just nothing but a demon," came a voice behind Jo -- it was the same one who had spoken to her earlier. In a flash, a white figure hovered over her and Dezmon as they were still in the air. By default, Dezmon let go of Jo's shirt and she fell quickly from above the auditorium stage. She screamed for help knowing that when she hit the ground, that was going to be it. Right before she was a foot from the impact, arms took hold of her and she was flying through the doors and straight into the janitor's closet in what felt like seconds. Jo saw that Axel was there as well, looking surprised when she got back on her feet. Turning around, she met the white figure that had shown up and rescued her from above. He seemed a few years older than her and his hair was naturally blonde, with light skin that seemed similar to Avy's. He wore something similar to Dezmon -- including the Converse they both wore -- but it was all white instead of black. And right behind him were a pair of wings that were so white, they almost seemed to glow.

As recognizable as Dezmon's face was, so was this boy's that stood in front of her. But she didn't dare say anything at first.

He walked over to Axel and with just his two hands, ripped the chains free. The only thing that didn't come off was the dark stain that was already on the chains and had outlined a circle around Axel's neck and wrists.

"This," said the boy in white to Axel, "will only come off if you believe that the chains are gone." Axel didn't say anything at all as the boy in white turned to Jo and asked, "Are you alright?"

"Who are *you*?" she questioned, hoping that she was partially right.

"I'm not important right now," he said as he kept exchanging looks between her and the door that was closed behind him. "I just need to know if you're okay."

"What's going on?" Jo asked.

"Okay, you're good then," the boy in white said. "Listen, you two," he started, referring to both Jo and Axel, "whatever you do, do *not* leave this room until I come back. Got it?"

"Uhh,"

"Good," he said already facing the door to leave.

"Wait!" Jo cried, which made the boy in white stop and turn around. "What's your name?"

The boy in white looked at Jo, then at Axel. "I go by Ozias."

Then Ozias went through the door, leaving the two in the janitor's closet.

***

"I can't take this anymore," Jo said, stopping herself from pacing anymore. It had been five minutes since Ozias had left the two in the janitor's closet, which was beyond disorganized. "I'm going to find him and ask this dude with wings what's going on."

"I think we should stay here," Axel stated, the first thing he ever said that was directed at her after he shot her. She faced him, unsure of what to say, but she looked away immediately before any interaction could be made between the two.

"How am I going to wake myself out of this?" Jo thought out loud. Axel turned to her with confusion on his face.

"What?" she asked him. "I'm going to find my way out of this. I have to eventually wake up from this strange dream that I'm in, and you're in, and umm...."

"Jo?" he asked her. "What are you talking about?"

"You know what I'm talking about," she told him. "None of this is real. That crazy psycho gothic guy isn't real and neither is Mr. White. This is all just some dream that I'll wake up from. You're not even real either. You're probably still in Texas letting me wonder where in the world has Axel Lardica been?"

Axel just looked at her like she was crazy or maybe he was confused about the whole him-being-in-her-dream. "Jo," he said carefully, "I get that you're scared of being here but.... this *is* real."

"I know it's not real," she denied, "because there's no way that my long lost best friend would ever go into my school and shoot me right in the heart without ever thinking it through."

"But Jo.... that's what happened," Axel told her weakly. "I really did kill you."

"You're lying... I don't believe it for a second that all of this is flat out real," she said, shaking her head.

"I'm not lying, Jo."

"You couldn't be the real Axel. No, the real Axel would never do that to me..." she protested, taking a few steps back from him.

"Jo, I'm really sorry," he said sincerely.

"NO!" she cried. "You're not him! You're not my Axel!"

"It's okay," he said, moving closer to her and trying to gently grab her arm.

"DON'T TOUCH ME!!" With anger, Jo shoved him back as hard as she could. "GET AWAY FROM ME!!" she said, voice cracking and wondering why she had tried to save him. "THE REAL AXEL WOULD NEVER BREAK HIS PROMISE!!"

With that, Jo went through the door and ran down the hall to find Ozias, leaving Axel in silence.

Chapter IV

Mortals with Immortals

The moving truck's rear door slammed shut with the last of Axel's things; all the things that made it home for Axel in this town that was stuck in a valley next to a military base. He had hoped this day would never come, ever since he found out about his parents separating from each other.

He didn't want to leave home. He had always thought he would live here forever and watch the place grow up with him. But his mother didn't want to stay in the place where she had fallen in love with his father. So she had randomly decided that their new home was going to be in Texas. She explained to ten-year-old Axel that it was about time they made new memories for themselves and start fresh.

But Axel wanted to make memories here in Georgia.

"It's time, kiddo," said his mother as the two movers disappeared into the moving truck that was parked in front of his house. "You ready to go?"

He wanted to say no, but he knew he couldn't.

His mother looked past him and smiled at what she saw. "Well, looks like someone's here to see you." Axel turned around and there she was.

Jo Silver.

His greatest, best friend who always had on a shirt about Shakespeare or a quote from books she loved. Her hair had always been either up in a ponytail or loose and she always wore Converse. The Converse's she wore that day were dark purple high tops.

"I always get a pair every year for my birthday," she had once told him. "It's kinda like a thing I always look forward to every year, changing from one pair of Converse to the next, from one color to another color. And sometimes, I like to keep some of them."

"What if you outgrow them?" Axel had once asked her.

"Then I outgrow them," Jo said casually, "Until you stop growing, you have to move on from what you had last year."

"Hey," she said to him, after crossing the street, "you thought you could try and get away without telling me goodbye?"

"Never," Axel said, smiling. "So, this is it then?"

"I wish it wasn't," she told him.

"I don't want to go," he admitted.

"I don't want you to go either, Axel. But maybe you have to go to the next pair of Converse without me," she explained before she quickly embraced him.

"Can you promise me something?" Jo whispered in his ear.

"Anything,"

"Promise me that you won't drift away?"

"I promise, Josephine Silver."

"Hey!" she said, pulling out from the hug to meet his eyes. "I go by 'Jo,' remember?"

"Who came up with that name?"

"I dunno," she shrugged, "some kid in the neighborhood."

They laughed right when Axel's mom called to him from the car, saying it was time for them to leave. The two went up to the car and he got in the passenger seat and rolled down the window as Jo stood at the car door.

"Oh, I almost forgot," Jo said, digging out a black bandana from her back pocket. "This is for you," she told him as she put it in his hand. "This is something to remember me by."

"Thanks," he said, already wrapping the bandana around his wrist.

"I have one too, see?" she said, showing hers on her wrist as well.

"So I wouldn't forget you."

"Glad you won't," then, in a whisper, so his mom wouldn't hear him, "because I'll be back one day and you'll be the first one I visit."

Jo smiled, then took a few steps away from the car. "Goodbye Axel."

"Bye Jo."

His mom moved their car forward as the moving truck followed behind. His eyes never left Jo Silver's eyes and she stood there until their car turned and vanished from sight.

I promise I won't drift away, Jo. Axel thought to himself, *I promise I'll come back soon.*

If only he had visited her sooner before he had drifted away.

***

It had been very painful watching Jo walk out of the janitor's closet fearing him. It was something he was used to from others but never from Jo Silver. In the years they had been friends, she had never really broken down like the way she did at that moment.

But he knew it was all because of him.

Axel Lardica had drifted away from home and from her, even though he had promised her he would never do it. It still happened. He left Georgia to live in Texas with his mom. He found himself with a step-father. Worst of all, he still saw himself pulling the trigger on Jo.

Axel finally made himself leave the janitor's room and walk down the hall to find Jo again. He had to find her and explain everything that brought him to this action.

Besides his footsteps on the tile floor, everything was silent. If Jo, Ozias, or even Dezmon were nearby, he couldn't hear any of them in the distance. The school seemed haunted now that everyone was gone.

A screech erupted down the halls and immediately Axel broke into a run.

DON'T TOUCH ME!! Jo screamed in his head as he was getting closer to the screeching. *THE REAL AXEL WOULD NEVER BREAK HIS*

PROMISE!! He honestly wouldn't have done that to her. Axel wasn't going to kill her. All he wanted to do was go see her, find her with her hair loose again, see her personality come to life, her new pair of Converse she would have. He never planned to even bring a gun.

But it was still his fault and he let it happen.

The screech came again and Axel stopped and listened carefully. Distant voices arose with a screech along with powerful thumps against what sounded like walls. Once Axel had an idea as to where it came from, he started running again, trying to get closer because if Ozias was there, then maybe Jo would be too. The screeches and slams directed him to the gymnasium and Axel caught a glimpse of the two black and white figures.

From what he could tell, Ozias and Dezmon fought each other differently. Ozias would do every move, every strong flap of his wings, every power as if his life depended on it; as if he thought he would fail if he didn't win against Dezmon. On the other hand, Dezmon enjoyed adding scars and blood on Ozias' all white outfit. The dark winged guy looked more like an animal with wings attacking than a natural human being. Every time Axel would look at Dezmon, he would panic just at the sight of the person that broke him. He was backing off from fear of seeing Dezmon when suddenly a figure bumped into him at full speed.

It was her.

"What the...?" she started, but Axel didn't let her finish when he put his hand over her mouth and pushed his body right beside the door frame with her body right against his. She didn't struggle when she heard Ozias and Dezmon talking to each together as they fought hard.

"I told you to stay away from him!" Ozias cried out in fury as he pushed Dezmon back with his legs while airborne. Dezmon hit the wall hard and was falling until his wings found air to fly again. "You were supposed to *never* lay hands on him!"

"I have the right to take them with me! It's not my problem if you couldn't handle two mortals on your own," Dezmon accused with an evil grin. "But you were too busy stalking..."

"YOU KEEP *HER* OUT OF THIS!" Ozias screamed. "SHE HAS NO PART IN ANY OF THIS!!!" Jo's body tensed up as their voices got louder and their bodies were thrown harder.

"You know darn well that she *is* a part of this," the black-winged boy told the white-winged boy as he flung himself at him, and brought him down hard on the basketball court -- making a loud booming sound that made Axel cringe. At this point, Ozias was pinned against the floor by Dezmon's arms and legs. "She, sure enough, is a part of this great plan I have made thanks to your help."

"You're lying just like any demon would," Ozias told him.

"Like any demon would," Dezmon mocked. "Is that what I am to you now?"

"It's what you've always been ever since those wings grew dark," Ozias pointed out.

"I'm glad. I enjoy ruining all your lives," Dezmon said, "because if I ruin the lives of all the mortals you watch over -- and hers -- I ruin your life as well."

Jo then broke free from Axel and bolted into the gym and, without even thinking about it, Axel followed behind. Dezmon was the first to lay eyes on the two as he said, "Well, looks like I've got all my game pieces together."

"What did I tell you guys?" Ozias yelled.

"I wasn't going to stand around and do nothing in a closet," Jo explained, crossing her arms.

"Mortals," mumbled Dezmon, as he suddenly charged at Jo but, before he could take hold of her, Axel pushed her out of the way and it was he that was grabbed again by Dezmon. The black-winged demon flung himself -- along with Axel -- up in the air and laughed hysterically as he pulled Axel close and wrapped his arm around him. The school shooter did his best to take breaths so he wouldn't pass out as he was hanging in the air. "Why do mortals think they can conquer the immortals, huh?"

"Put him down!" Ozias warned.

"Maybe it's because they have no idea what the afterlife's really like until they've reached the other side. Right? They have no idea how much more powerful we are."

"Drop him, Dezmon!" Ozias cried. "Drop him before I send you back down to Hell myself!"

"This isn't over!" Dezmon proclaimed. He randomly threw Axel from his grip and in a flash, Ozias caught him in midair. A hole had then formed through the basketball court's floor and was getting large enough to fit any of them, almost like a portal. Inside the hole was pure darkness as the demonic winged beast kid fell from midair and went into the portal. The opening of the portal vanished immeiately and was back to a normal court floor.

Ozias brought Axel back down to the ground and then looked at the two in exasperation. "Are you two serious?"

"What?" Jo asked.

"I did not need your help," Ozias stated. "I needed you safe. If the two of you aren't safe, then things won't end well."

"Why do *we* have to be safe?" Axel asked.

"Can you please tell us what's going on?" Jo begged. "I'm tired of not knowing what's really happening. I don't even know who you are."

"You wanna know?" Ozias asked, "Name's Ozias. I'm an angel. You met Dezmon, who's obviously a demon and his job is to bring you two back with him. I stopped him and now you're both here. There, I explained. Happy? Now we have to go before Dezmon comes back with his buddies."

Ozias walked out of the gymnasium as Axel and Jo followed without saying another word.

Chapter V

Crime Scene

Ozias would casually look back every so often at the two mortals, making sure they were actually following him -- which thankfully, they were. Both of them were confused and probably scared of all the things that could happen in the afterlife because it wasn't every day you see a demon fight with an angel for mortals like them.

And that was the problem— those two weren't supposed to see any of that. Once their heartbeat stopped or they lost enough blood, they were supposed to go where they belong eternally.

Hell.

But Ozias knew he couldn't let them go with Dezmon. The angel had a feeling that those two weren't supposed to die so soon. He never got a report or warning about them having to die soon and usually, angels get some kind of warning from above about it. The only thing he could think of as to why they'd died so young all led to Dezmon.

She, sure enough, is a part of this great plan I have made thanks to your help. Ozias kept repeating what Dezmon had told him over and over in his head -- trying to figure out what plan he was trying to fulfill with not only Jo and Axel but with *her* as well.

"I'm not going to let him do that," he mumbled.

"What?" Jo asked.

"Nothing," Ozias replied, "Just thinking."

"So, umm," Jo started, "I wasn't sure how to ask this because I might be crazy too and it kinda is crazy umm because you look so much like what I had imagined you guys to be -- kind of -- and, well..." Ozias stopped and turned around to look at her trying to ask the question he already knew about, but he decided to let her finish it. "Okay, if you're Ozias and Dezmon was the other guy, who is Abaddon and E.J. here?"

He sighed, picturing both figures in his mind and said, "Abaddon and E.J. are very well known here -- two of the greatest friends since the beginning of time -- before the Earth was even made. They were once the symbol of true friendship for all of Heaven and were two of the greatest immortals here," he stated, not sure if he should continue.

"So does that mean they're around here then? Just waiting to come out or what?" Jo urged, wanting to know more about them.

"You seriously think we're your *characters* in your book?" he asked right off the bat.

"Well, isn't that what this is? My own conscience and he --," she referred to Axel, "is a part of my memories and you and Dezmon are a part of it because I mentally created you?" she asked, crossing her arms, "because I'm not dead?"

Ozias couldn't believe Jo Silver, the girl he had watched over since birth, was denying the fact that she -- as a matter of fact -- *was* dead. She thinks it's all some dream and that this was all inside her head and the rest of them were just playing some game with their "creator."

"You are dead, Jo."

"No, I'm not dead," she replied firmly. "I'm inside my head as I wait in this dream for Monday to come."

"This is real, Jo," Ozias said slowly, trying to stay as calm as possible. "This is as real as it can be."

"'Cause I'm inside my own head," Jo argued. "If I'm inside my head, I must be dreaming..."

"Josephine Silver," Ozias said, holding her shoulders firmly. "Listen to me right now."

"I have to wake up."

"Jo..."

Jo's hands covered her face as she kept repeating her sentence. "This is all just a dream." Ozias looked at her, then at Axel, who was looking at Jo as if he was trying to figure out how he could explain all of this to her because surely he got the memo that they were both dead.

"Jo," Axel said, touching her shoulder. "Look at me, okay?"

She did with hopeful, yet still fearful eyes. Ozias figured if an angel couldn't get through to her, maybe her long-lost friend could. "I know this is really hard to accept, but we're not in a dream. We're both dead and I know it's my fault we got into this mess and I'm sorry....." Axel stopped and Ozias knew immediately why. There were sirens blaring from outside of the building and it sounded as if a S.W.A.T. team had arrived at the school. "Oh no!" he said in horror.

"We need to leave now!" Ozias said, taking both of the mortals' arms and running before they could even say a word. His halfway outstretched wings were catching air. In a flash motion, he jerked the two close to his body, wrapping one arm around their waists firmly as they struggled to keep up with his pace and stay close to him at the same time.

"Are you *insane?*" Jo yelled.

"We have to get away before..." Ozias' heart was pumping fast as he heard the familiar screeching sounds of multiple demons nearby. Without another word, Ozias extended his wings and with a big flap, he -- along with the two mortals – went up through the ceiling and roof of the school, into the sunshine and blue sky above them.

Ozias looked down to his left to see Axel looking out in amazement at the sky as the angel hovered above -- seeing the clouds as if they had never existed before. His face changed when the mortal looked down, seeing the multiple flashes of lights from all the police and S.W.A.T. team cars and trucks, frowning at the realization that he was the cause of it all. Jo's head was hidden in Ozias' side as she was breathing forcefully. Ozias knew she was doing her best not to freak out about being so high up in the air, so he glided down and landed gracefully in front of the school's main entrance.

"Jo."

"Yeah?" Jo asked, petrified.

"We're on the ground," Ozias replied, trying to speak over the blaring of the sirens that surrounded the three of them. Jo opened her eyes and saw the many police cars and trucks along with the entire school, altogether in a clump away from the school building. Breaking off from Ozias' hold on her, she slowly walked closer to the frightened living people. She seemed shocked as she looked into the faces of the crowd as if looking for an answer to this madness.

Axel was in a haze, knowing that all of this was because of him. Ozias gently touched his shoulder to comfort him, knowing that there was a lot going on in his head. The mortal boy still stood there, looking like he wanted to grieve over his own doing -- over his own death. "One person did all of this," he whispered to himself, but Ozias still heard it.

"Axel..."

"One person caused all this mess."

"Just try to..."

"I should've fought it," he suddenly said hysterically, inhaling and exhaling like he couldn't breathe. Ozias tried to calm him down but when Axel looked at his wrist and saw the stains from the black chains, he grew worse. His panic brought him to the floor as he started to rock himself back and forth, repeating the same sentence. The angel tried to snap him out of it, but the mortal wouldn't respond to anything Ozias was trying to tell him.

This wasn't as easy as Ozias had expected.

"Jo!" Ozias cried, going up to her as she stood watching the crowd of people before her. "I need you to help calm Axel before things get worse around here."

Jo said nothing, still scanning this dramatic scene of police officers giving out orders to both their team, the teenagers, and teachers from the school. There were a lot of voices filling everyone's ears with commands as well as screams and sobbing. Ozias hoped she would realize this wasn't a dream. It was harsh to think like that but the angel knew if worst came to worst, he had to make sure she would understand what's really going on.

"Jo," Ozias said softly, "Axel needs you right now."

She still wouldn't reply, her stone-like face toward the crowd.

"Silver,"

"You don't exist," she said, "You're just a made up character in my head who is trying to tell me this whole nightmare is real...that watching my best friend mourn for me is real..." Ozias looked out at the crowd and found the mortal's friend crying so hard, it looked like her world was falling apart -- and it surely was. The immortal was conflicted about the things that mortals think and how they don't sometimes understand what really happens in situations like this. He looked at the girl with the most beautiful natural blonde hair— always in a bun, her face with makeup she really never needed, and tears streaming down her face. The angel hated to see her in tears -- especially now that she was starting to look lost.

"Can you just talk to him?" he finally said, still staring at the lost friend in tears.

"He's a memory," Jo replied, "I can't do anything about it."

"Tell me something, Jo," Ozias started, "if Axel really is a memory of yours, wouldn't you see him as the ten-year-old Axel who left the summer before middle school -- entirely right before you met her?" He asked, referring to Avy.

Jo pressed her lips together as if trying to find her version of an answer to this. But there was no time for her to reply when a loud, screeching sound suddenly was heard, taking the sky from blue to black as dark figures. There were maybe about six or seven of them so far, but enough to take the mortals down. Ozias didn't hesitate as he took her arm and ran towards Axel -- forcing him to get up and run from the demons that has found their prey.

"Where are we going?" Jo cried, trying to keep up her pace next to Ozias and Axel.

"Safest place is your house," the angel replied. "Do not stop, go straight there and leave them to me," he commanded, hoping they would actually listen this time.

"What are you going to do?" Jo huffed, trying to fill her lungs with air.

"To fly, of course," the angel replied, spreading his wings out and with a big flap, Ozias was airborne.

Chapter VI

Flying Demons or Flying Monkeys?

Jo was barely able to keep up with Axel -- who was already out of breath right away after seeing all the demons flying above them. Running had never been her strong suit and her calves were feeling it.

After Ozias took flight to fight against the demons that were there, Jo and Axel were racing down J.R. Allen Parkway heading towards her house from school. Usually, the school bus would drive them down this highway instead of her and Axel running down it in some dream she was having. By car, her house was less than five minutes away -- but now she couldn't tell how long it would take to get to her house. The highway wasn't busy since it was early in the afternoon. If she were "awake" and had done this crazy stunt of running down the highway, she would have already been dead by the few cars going through her "ghostly" figure.

From above, she could hear the demons trying to toy with her and Axel from their dark, not-so-comforting voices, saying things like, "You're nothing now that you're here," "You'll never make it in this life," "Just let yourself fall to Hell." It sounded like suicidal thoughts.

Jo turned back to find Dezmon among the demons that had shown up and were all fighting against Ozias. From the ground, hearing their mockery and sneers, Jo thought the demons looked like flying monkeys from *The Wizard of Oz* which almost made her laugh. Jo could've been the tougher version of Dorothy with Axel as the Tin Man, and a white smart flying monkey who was Ozias. Then at this thought, she had to laugh again.

By then, her legs should've been stinging but they somehow weren't even hurting that much. It was as if she couldn't fully feel herself. Even trying to catch her breath wasn't as difficult as it should've been, yet, it wasn't.

At that point, they were a quarter of a mile away from the exit leading to Moon Road -- the road that would take them to her house. Both Jo and Axel glanced at the same time towards the sky -- seeing that there were fewer demons there than before. It was actually Dezmon who was left fighting with Ozias. But in a split second, Axel's face went from exhaustion to alarm.

"They're *diving!*" he cried right before he shoved Jo out of the way -- making the two mortals topple over each other on the grass beside the road, rolling a few times before their momentum could be stopped. Ozias' body was physically shoved to the ground from the sky by Dezmon -- making the angels backslide against the hard cement. Blood was on both the black and the white figures as they continued to fight as hard as previously at the school gym.

"They belong to me!" Dezmon screeched as his sharp nails marked blood on Ozias.

"Those two were *never* yours!" the angel replied firmly, shoving the demon off of him and standing again. With his back facing the mortals and his front facing Dezmon, both Jo and Axel saw all that the cement had done to the angel's back and wings, marking him with scrapes and cuts that ranged from mild to severe. "Now I am saying it again. LEAVE BEFORE I SEND YOU BACK TO HELL MYSELF!" Ozias snarled.

"You have no idea how much fun I'm gonna have with you when I ruin everything you care about," the demon chuckled as he ascended above and disappeared in the blink of an eye.

Now, there was only the wounded angel with the two mortals who said nothing for the longest time until finally, the angel started limping his way down Moon Road.

"Come on," he said painfully, "we need to get home before more demons come." Jo looked at Axel who was still looking at the angel's wounded back and blood-stained wings. He was struggling to walk and they knew that.

As they followed, the angel did his best to walk as normally as possible. but deep down inside Jo knew he was hurting badly because of them.

**

Ozias was doing his best not to drag his feet on the cement but you could hear his pure white Converses being scraped from the bottom.

Axel couldn't believe that the angel -- with basically his entire body scraped up and stained with blood -- was still keeping his head high as he dragged his limp leg. It was like he didn't even want to take care of himself or ask Jo or Axel for help.

"Ozias," he called weakly.

The angel stopped the scraping of his shoe and turned to face him. "Yeah?"

"I shouldn't be here."

"Neither of you should be here," the angel told him, "But I... Axel know."

"Know what?" the boy asked confused.

"You can't think like that here, okay? Any demon could haunt you just by the thoughts you think."

"What are you talking about?" the mortal asked, confused.

The angel pointed at his temple. "I'm an angel, I hear mortals' thoughts all the time."

"What!" Jo proclaimed, "So you mean to tell me I have no privacy in my head?"

"I hear what needs to be heard," Ozias answered. "I've been with you two ever since you were born."

"Yeah, okay," Jo scuffed. "Like you know all my..."

"You were obsessed with Blue's Clues and presently you still watch the shows."

"HOW DARE YOU SAY THAT IN PUBLIC?" she roared in shock. "How would you know that?"

"Well," he started, "I was a guardian angel to both of you."

Jo laughed while Axel was confused by what Ozias was trying to say. "That was a good one, oh!" came back Jo. Axel had no idea how she could be acting like this. Does she really think that all of this is just....

"You think this is funny?" Ozias asked.

"You think you're our *guardian angel*," she said as if it made sense. "You're just a character of mine who thinks you can protect us."

"THAT'S IT!" boomed the angel louder than anyone else would as he went up to her. "Let me tell you something—I'M NOT SOME CHARACTER FROM *YOUR* UNTOLD STORY. *OKAY?* THIS ISN'T SOME DREAM, JO. I'M REALLY YOUR GUARDIAN ANGEL WHO SAW AND HEARD IT ALL. I FOUGHT EVERY DAY -- EV-RY-DAY -- LIKE THIS FOR YOU BOTH FOR YEARS. YOU THINK IT WAS EASY TO WATCH YOU TWO DO THINGS YOU SHOULD-N'T, BE SOMETHING YOU SHOULDN'T? I DO MY BEST TO TRY AND KEEP YOU OUT OF HARM'S WAY OR ELSE MY ENTIRE JOB IS A WASTE."

"Well, if this were real, you would've already failed at it then," Jo answered, as if she didn't understand what the angel was trying to say. "We're 'dead,' Ozias! So I think if all of this were real you would've already sucked at the job. And aren't angels always supposed to be happy—all the time, and tell whomever they're always going to be okay?"

"Jo!" Axel jumped in, "Why would you say that after all he's done to himself for us?" the boy said, referring to the blood and scrapes on the once white angel.

"No," the angel stopped him, "she's right. I didn't do my job and Dezmon was able to do this. I didn't fight hard enough for you two."

"Dezmon mentioned about having the right to take us," Jo stated in all seriousness, then. "What's that about?"

The angel sighed, "When you die if you didn't already believe, the demons have the right to take you back to Hell with them."

"We were supposed to go to *Hell?*" she asked slowly.

Ozias nodded.

"So why didn't we?"

"I knew I shouldn't," Ozias started, "But I knew something wasn't right and that Dezmon was -- in some way -- a part of both of your deaths and I wouldn't let him take you two. I had to know what really happened before they sent you down there."

"So you took us from him and ran?" Axel questioned.

"For now until I know what's really going on."

"What about 'she?'" Jo asked, "Dezmon mentioned a 'she'. Who is it?"

"C'mon," the angel said, dragging his feet again, "we have to keep moving." "Ozias," Jo called, but the whole walk to her house, Ozias never told her who the "she" was the demon mentioned.

Chapter VII

Grieving from the Living and the Dead

If it weren't for the many hills that basically made up her neighborhood, Jo would've already been at the house ages ago. They eventually made it -- hours later -- to her ranch-style white brick home on Wimbish Court -- on one of the most inclined hills they could ever walk up. Next to her mailbox stood a giant cherry blossom tree Jo had always had growing up. The tree had been there longer than she had, but Jo always knew she would come back to find the tree still blooming in the spring and summer, and watch it fade away in the fall and winter. No matter what, it would always be there.

"Wow," mumbled Axel, "I thought I'd never come back here."

"I always saw us as kids hanging out around here whenever I stood outside." Jo told him, "It was like replaying a memory, I guess."

"I wish I did that before," Axel mumbled to himself.

"Let's hurry and get inside before Dezmon comes back." Ozias was crossing the yard towards the front door. The two mortals followed and all three went inside, landing in the living room area of the house. For some reason, Jo felt something seemed different when she was inside her home. It was like it was her home, but she didn't fully think it was.

"So now what?" Jo asked as Axel scanned his eyes around the place as if he was trying to remember it again.

"Now," Ozias said, "We..."

From the window, Jo could see two cars pulling into her driveway at the same time. She recognized her dad's Jetta and mom's Kia. "My parents are here!" she exclaimed, going out to greet them until a hand stopped her.

"Jo," Ozias said cautiously. "You need to understand something."

"What?" Jo asked, "They're my parents. I'm sure they can handle you two."

"It's not your parents that I'm worried about," Ozias said, looking at the side door as both her father and mother came through it. Jo turned around in joy, only to change her face to confusion.

"Mom? Dad?" she called with worry in her voice. Her parents walked through the door, both looking weary and depressed. Without noticing Jo, her mother sat down on the couch without saying a word as her father sat down next to her. Jo took a few steps closer, hoping her appearance had caught their eye. She called to her parents again, but neither responded to her.

"She's gone," Jo's mother told her husband with tears filling her eyes.

"Ellie...." Jo's father put his arm around her.

"My baby's gone!" her mother sobbed, sinking into Jo's father as tears rushed down her face.

"Mom! I'm here!" Jo cried out, "It's okay, I'm right here." She walked closer to her parents and tried to touch them for comfort, but the mortal saw that even to her own parents she was an invisible ghostly figure. Her mother -- along with her father -- wept and wept because of Jo and she tried everything to tell them she was okay and was right there with them. But they did not hear a single word that came out of her mouth and it was breaking her apart on the inside so badly she started to cry herself.

How could this possibly happen that they thought she had died? What kind of dream was this?

Jo -- with tears running down her face -- looked at the boys who were watching all of this, wondering if all of this wasn't some kind of dream. It was starting to feel too real for her and she was deeply scared that this was actually her death story. She looked at Axel, realizing that Ozias' statement of him not being a memory was true. Jo had not seen Axel since the time his car and the moving truck drove away from her as she'd waved goodbye. Suddenly, she stormed towards her childhood best friend -- with Ozias stopping her before she got to him -- and cried out in fury. "THIS IS ALL YOUR FAULT!!!"

His face showed that he knew he was the cause of all of this. Maybe he knew all along it was his fault that he physically shot her on purpose only to shoot himself right after. It had shown many times before when she thought this all seemed to be untrue -- but Axel knew all along this was real. Even Ozias knew this was not some dream. He was an angel, for crying out loud! He'd fought demons for the two only to continue harming his body, and for what? Still with Jo thinking that he was some character in her untold story?

Why was she so stupid?

Maybe because she hoped this was the key to ending her writer's block and maybe write a decent story for the first time ever. But it was already too late. She had lost her.....

"Ozias," she managed to say, feeling her body go limp for some reason. "I can't feel anything." Jo fell into his embrace as he kept hold of her. Her body was suddenly starting to hurt mostly towards her back.

"Jo, are you okay?" the angel asked. "What's going on?"

"M-My back... it hurts," she said, as the pain grew stronger. "It hurts, Ozias. It's really hurting." It was hard to think of words to speak because the pain grew stronger and stronger and it was starting to become difficult to hear her parents weeping and Ozias' voice above her. Ozias picked her up in a log carry style and raced to the kitchen and out the back door. Ozias brought her -- with Axel trailing right behind -- into the shed at the bottom of the Silver's inclined backyard. By the time Ozias laid her down, Jo felt something in her back and she had to get it out immediately before the pain grew stronger. Her arms reached behind her, trying to find out what was back there.

"Jo? Listen to me, okay?" came the angel's voice, "You're going to be fine. Just relax for me and it'll go away. I promise....."

"Ozias," Jo heard Axel's voice come in, sounding in pain as well. The angel turned to find Axel on the floor shaking violently from something. The angel left Jo's side to go to Axel and in that moment she got hold of a small stub of something near her shoulder blades. The point of it felt smooth and seemed to be dug deep into her back. She knew she had to find out what was going on with her -- why she was feeling all this pain right now.

So Jo took a good hold on it and started to pull it out slowly.

Every time she started to pull it out, she would have some kind of memory from her past pop up. Jo learning to ride a bike, her first word she spoke, the first day of middle school, meeting Avy, fun time with her parents, finding out that Axel was leaving, then returning with a gun pointed at her.

Maybe it was like what people say— while you are dying, you go back to your life and replay it before your very eyes. Between memories, she saw Ozias trying to help Axel but the boy was shaking so hard, it looked like he was having a seizure.

The thing she was pulling out was still in her but it was hard to even tell what it was until she saw it with her very eyes.

When Ozias spoke to her, his voice was muffled in her ears and very distant. "Jo! Are you okay? Say something for me!"

Jo tried to say something but nothing came out when she opened her mouth. She was only able to focus on her hand, pulling whatever was inside of her out, hoping the pain would go away somehow. Her body started shivering as she started to feel light headed.

No, she thought. She had to see what was hurting her. *Almost there, J. just keep pulling.*

Finally, she felt relief as whatever had been in her back was now gone. Pulling her arm in front of her again, she saw a large size.... feather?

It was stained with blood -- perhaps her own -- but she could tell that the color of it was grayish. It wasn't as white as Ozias', nor was it as dark as Dezmon's. But it was a feather, a feather that came straight from her back.

Ozias rushed to her side with his wings blocking her view of Axel an his condition. "Jo, can you hear me? Are you...."

Jo couldn't say anything really. It felt too heavy to say anything. All she was able to do was hand the single gray blood-stained feather to Ozias' and fall back into darkness.

Chapter VIII

The Unknown is Now Known

Go find her, said that voice inside of him repetitively.

He sat in his truck knowing this was a bad idea. It had always been a bad idea from the start, but it seemed as if his own mind was being forced to do this. He shouldn't be here. He should be with his mom, hoping the snake of the house wouldn't hurt her while he was gone.

Don't you miss her? The voice inside of him asked. Of course, he did. He'd missed seeing her every day after school for the next adventure they would have. This voice inside him had urged him to drive all the way to the military town from Texas—to do what exactly? Just go up to her to say hi? Hoping that she didn't forget him in all these years of being apart?

What if she forgot about him? What if she didn't remember the bandana she had given him before? Would she be easily recognizable? Or would he find her different from the memories he had of her?

"I shouldn't be here," he whispered to himself, already worried about his mother who was in the hands of the Snake. He should be protecting his mom from his own stepfather instead of being selfish and coming back to his hometown to find one girl.

Go find her, the voice told him again. *You came all this way to start over and have a second chance -- with her -- and you want to back out now?* The voice was right. He wanted to have a second chance with her in it. But looking at the gun in his hands, he knew this wasn't right. This never felt like the right thing to do to get a second chance.

"I can't do this," he said, part of it to himself and part of it to the voice inside of him.

Of course, you can. The voice said as if this was an easy task. *You know how to use it, so all you have to do is find her.*

"No! I can't do that to her. I can't.."

Yes, you can, Axel. The voice urged.

"I don't want to do this anymore. I don't want this..."

YOU ARE GOING TO DO IT! The voice boomed inside of him, as he felt his head throbbing unnaturally. He tried to fight it, but the pain made him feel weaker.

"Okay! Okay! I'll do it! Just please stop!"

What a wise choice. The voice commented, and his pain went away. *Now go before it's too late.*

Axel got out of his truck with the gun tucked inside of his pants underneath his shirt and jacket. He nervously walked towards the school, knowing there was no way out of this madness inside of him. It was now or never.

"I hope you'll forgive me, Josephine Silver," he whispered to himself, knowing he would never forgive himself for this.

***

Jo woke up to the sound of Ozias' voice praying. It sounded like he was reciting The Lord's Prayer -- or so Jo thought. Relieved she had no more pain; she slowly tried to get up from the shed floor.

"Oh, glad you woke up," Ozias told her after he finished with an Amen. "Are you in pain?"

"No," she said quickly, looking around the shed. "How long has it been?"

"Two human days,"

"Two *days?*" she repeated in astonishment.

"Yes, it's Wednesday." Ozias stated, "Your funeral is this Saturday at noon. Avy has offered to do your eulogy and the pastor that baptized you when you were younger is speaking there as well."

Jo was quiet. She then remembered where she really was. She

wasn't in some stupid dream; she was dead among the living. She hadn't believed that she was dead until she'd watched her own parents grieve for her. "Where's Axel?" she inquired.

"He's out on the swing set," Ozias replied nervously, changing glances between her and whatever was behind her.

"Well, aren't you supposed to be -- oh I don't know -- making sure he doesn't get caught by some pack of demons?"

"Well, of course." the angel answered her in a matter-of-fact tone. "But it's not him I'm worried about right now."

"What do you mean?"

The angel went up to her and knelt close enough for her to hear his tender whisper. "Just don't freak out, okay?"

"Yeah, sure," she said, nervous about what Ozias was doing. The angel took her hand and helped her stand to her feet. Then he guided her to the one mirror in the entire shed that was one of the antiques her father had purchased years before. She was little when they got it and still remembered the day they both found that interesting mirror. It was oval shaped and was covered in dust. But what made this mirror any different from all the other mirrors was the roman key symbol placed right at the top. When her father was paying for it, the cashier had told them -- mostly to the young Jo -- that the key unlocks a whole new world that's greater than this one.

"A world of imagination," she emphasized to her. "And that key will always take you there."

Ozias stopped before she saw her reflection through it. "When you see it, just try not to panic, okay?"

"See what?"

"Just trust me on this one."

"Okay," she replied as Ozias brought her in front of the keyed mirror. Reflecting back at her was Jo Silver wearing a t-shirt, high waist shorts, leggings, and red Converses. But this wasn't the same Jo Silver that lived in a military town in Georgia. This wasn't the Jo Avy had met. No, this Jo was someone else.

This Jo had *wings*.

They were as enormous as the wings on Ozias' back but they

weren't fully white or black. They had grayish colored feathers. Putting her arm back, she was able to feel the soft feathers for herself and know how real this all was.

"How...?"

"I wish I knew how," Ozias said, "but this seems impossible to comprehend."

"Wait, does this mean Axel...?"

"Yes."

"Is he okay?" she asked, still looking at herself in the mirror in awe and partially nervous.

"You should go see him," the angel encouraged, which surprisingly, Jo did. She walked out of the shed to find Axel with wings of his own, sitting on one of the swings. It was shocking to find that he wasn't going through the swing. Jo went up the tiny ladder of her childhood swing set and sat on top of her small slide without falling through. Neither of them said a word to each other and mostly it was because Axel was focused on the ground and Jo didn't know what to say.

He had killed her with just a single bullet. She *should* be furious with him right now. She should tell him to his face it was his fault they got into this mess and how they ended up having wings. But she didn't -- she couldn't because looking at her long lost friend, there was more to the story than what she had seen.

"Axel?"

"You don't have to talk to me," he replied. "I get it."

"What happened to you, Axel?"

"Everything happened."

"Axel."

"What?"

"What happened to the Axel I had to say goodbye to five years ago?"

He sighed. "We were fine -- my mom and I -- in Texas until I started school. Middle school sucked for me."

"It sucked for me too," she commented, "But I wasn't alone."

"Well I was," he said. "I kept thinking the next day would be a better one -- but it never was. My mom ended up marrying someone else and the day he moved in with us, we realized what his true colors were. Every day, I would wake up hoping he wasn't drunk and beating my mom up. Many times I knew I had to save her from it and bear the pain instead. It's been like that for awhile now."

He stopped for a moment and for sure Jo thought he wouldn't say any more, but he did. "Then I kept hearing a voice inside of me, telling me there's a whole new place to start over from. The voice kept saying I have the way to get there and you can take someone with you. Once the voice said how I had to get to that starting over place, I knew it wasn't a good idea. But when I rejected the offer, my head started to throb so hard, I could barely think."

He stopped again as if wondering whether to continue telling Jo or not. He made a decision quickly to continue. "I left Sunday night -- leaving a note for my mom -- and drove that whole night from Texas to here. The whole way, I kept telling myself I shouldn't be doing this, that I should be there protecting my mom. But every time I tried to go back, the pain in my head kept hurting until I got here. When the school bell rang, I knew this shouldn't be happening and I was regretting coming like this. But the voice insisted to go find you and if I didn't, he would give me more pain."

"That's why you were saying you were sorry," Jo pointed out. "It wasn't you who was really the school shooter. It was the voice in your head that made you do it." Jo thought about it and realized something else. "Dezmon was that voice, wasn't he?"

Axel nodded. "After I shot myself -- because I hated myself for pulling the trigger on you -- I woke up with the chains already on me and he was there." Axel rubbed his wrists that still had the stained black dust from the chains on them. "Ozias said I had to believe that they're off in order for the stains to go away."

"Do you?" she asked.

"Do I what?"

"Do you believe you are still in those chains?"

Axel shook his head. "I'm sorry Jo," he said. "I really am sorry for doing it."

"It's okay," she said quietly. "I forgive you."

"You do?"

"Yeah," she replied, "I do."

***

Night fell upon them quickly as all three went into the shed so the demons couldn't find them. None of them felt led to sleep so they decided to play Truth or Dare. Axel and Jo would always pick dare but the angel would always pick truth. The game had gotten pretty intense for the two mortals and they failed to ask why the angel didn't want to dare himself.

"Truth or Dare?" Jo asked Ozias.

"Truth," he replied.

Jo was trying to think of a question, but she didn't have to think long because this one question kept popping into her head for some reason, "Are you really an angel?"

"Woah!" came Axel, looking like he hadn't had this much fun in years.

The angel was thinking about it for a long time before he answered. "I wasn't at first."

"What?" Axel asked, sounding rather thrown off by this.

"You're not an angel?" Jo asked him confused. "But you have the wings, and the clothes and the job..."

"Yeah, now I do," Ozias agreed, "but I wasn't one at first."

"What do you mean?" she urged.

The angel sighed, changing his expression. "I'm an Unborn Angel."

"What does that mean?" Axel asked him. "There's more than one type of angel?"

Ozias chuckled for a moment. "Yeah, there're different kinds."

"So what makes you an Unborn Angel?" Jo asked, letting go of Truth or Dare for this new discovery.

"Well, I actually could've been living, I could've been alive." the angel started, "My parents couldn't wait to have me. They were excited I was on my way here and were very prepared for what was in store for them. I was excited as well. I watched them prepare my room and have the baby shower, and count off the days till I would come into the world like everyone else. They already had my name planned out and everything. I was going to be their firstborn."

"So what happened?" Jo asked, encouraging him to continue.

"A few months into the pregnancy my heartbeat stopped and the doctors weren't able to save me."

"Wait," Axel came. "So an Unborn Angel is a...."

"A miscarriage baby?" finished Ozias, "Yeah, that was me."

"Oh," Jo said quietly. "I'm sorry."

"So how'd you get the wings?" Axel asked.

"Well, an angel from Heaven asked what I wanted to do and I've always enjoyed watching angels help people here so I told him that I wanted to be an angel. So here I am," he said, presenting his wings in a funny matter which made both Axel and Jo laugh.

"So," Jo said, "are most angels Unborn Angels?"

"Not many," the angel replied. "They're mostly Unwished-For Angels."

"What are those?" Axel asked.

"Aborted kids."

"Oh."

"Actually, Dezmon is an Unwished-For Angel."

"*WHAT?*" came both mortals.

"He was an *angel?*"

"Well," the angel started, "to be more specific, he's an Unwished-For *Fallen* Angel."

"Fallen angels are demons," Jo had concluded. "I can't picture that at all."

"How do you know all of this?" Axel asked the angel.

"Ummm, I think we should..."

"*NO!*" both mortals exclaimed.

"Okay, okay," Ozias said, looking really surprised that they wanted to know. "Well, I was about a few months in before coming over here and I was hanging out with my parents for the day when I ran into him at an ice cream shop -- in a ghostly way -- and we kinda clicked. He was new because his mom had just gotten pregnant with him so I be-came— I guess a big brother to him and showed him what life was going to be like here. At that time, he didn't have a name, so I called him Daniel. Neither of us could wait to come down here until he watched his sixteen-year-old mother end his way here."

"That must've been hard for him to actually watch it," Jo said, trying her best to picture Dezmon's wings as white as Ozias' but could-n't.

"For days, he wouldn't come down with me to check on his mom. I thought it was because he needed to think about things. But what I did-n't know was that he had a lot of hate on the inside towards his mother and he let that sit inside him for a long time. By the time I realized he wasn't himself anymore, it was around the time he and I had become an-gels. I had talked him into becoming one and when I did, I realized I did-n't really know him anymore. He was saying how this whole 'Heaven' deal was just a bunch of crap and how there was no point in it." Ozias' face changed deeply as if he was remembering the entire thing. "He then attacked me about how perfect I was to everyone and how being an angel was what I would've done anyway. I tried to calm him down but he wouldn't and that was when he charged at me head on. That was when we had our first big fight."

"So then what?" asked Axel softly.

"His wings went from white to black and I had to push him off and he fell from Heaven," the angel said, bringing in a deep void. "I never saw him as white as he was again and he's hated me since."

It was hard to think that there's a whole other life on the other side with all the things that happened. The miscarriage babies get a sec-ond chance, the abortion children have a difficult recovery, fallen angels really do fall. It seemed there was always something for the things people never think about.

"What happened to his parents?"

Ozias sighed. "His dad left the picture to attend college before his mom could say anything about her pregnancy. She was stuck with the pressure and convinced herself that she couldn't do it alone. When I watch over you guys, I always see her around. She's your bus driver for school."

"What?" she said, "It can't be Mrs. Maine. No way."

"That's her," Ozias confirmed. Mrs. Maine? A mother of a psychopath demon that managed to kill them both? She couldn't understand the resemblance between the situation and the two.

"What about the dad?"

"I haven't seen him since he left. I don't think he knew about Dezmon's existence at all -- let alone his abortion," the angel explained.

"What about your family?" Axel asked him, "You didn't tell us what happened to them."

"If I do, would you go to sleep?" the angel asked sounding tired. Both mortals nodded, already laying down to get some rest. The angel did the same and waited for a few moments before he finally spoke again. Jo was on the verge of drifting to sleep without hearing it from himself who Ozias was related to. "They had a daughter two years later who they were still prepared for. She wouldn't remember me when she was here but I told her that I'll always be right here if she ever needed me."

"Who's your sister?" Jo whispered, her eyes struggling to keep open.

Jo thought she heard Ozias wrong about his sister's name. She could've sworn he mixed it up or said it the wrong way. But Jo couldn't protest or anything since right after she heard the name, she went into a deep sleep -- hoping that she didn't get the name wrong as it stuck in her head.

"Avy Whitman," Ozias' voice whispered.

Chapter IX

Dance the Night Away

Axel couldn't believe it was already Friday.

Ozias had been working with them on both his and Jo's flying along with some fighting skills since Thursday morning. The fighting was easy to master for the two since Axel had taught Jo a few things he learned growing up. It was a matter of learning what to do and how to do it. It came naturally to him once he learned the way things go.

Flying was an interesting lesson on the other hand. They practiced going down Jo's extremely inclined hill her house was on top of. The goal was to get a running start and continue that momentum until you attempted to take flight. It took Axel about five tries before he finally got it. Once he was up, he was amazed at how differently the world looked.

But Jo was struggling with flying. It was mostly because of her fear of heights. She would try and make an excuse for not doing it, or she would say that maybe she should do it later. When she was finally forced to learn, she couldn't get up off the ground without hurting herself. So Ozias would give her a break, knowing she would learn soon.

"I never wanted wings in the first place," Jo mumbled as she passed Axel for her next attempt, going up the hill for the millionth time.

"You got this, Jo!" Ozias encouraged. "Just relax and let it come naturally to you."

"Nothing that we're doing is natural!" Jo hollered back from the top of the hill. She was still looking at Ozias as if trying to picture Avy and Ozias being siblings.

"Let's go, Jo!" Axel exclaimed.

He saw her small smile right before she started her run down the hill. Her face said she was thinking about what Ozias had told her to do. *Make a good running start, and look ahead. When you're ready, jump up and flap hard.* Jo was halfway down the hill when she leaped off and tried to flap. It always happened that she was scared to flap her wings so she couldn't fly or it was really hard for her to actually get up there. But either way, Ozias still caught her before she ever touched a single toe on the pavement.

"I'll give you a break on that," the angel said to her. "You're improving a lot."

"What's the point?" she asked him. "I'm scared of heights and I have wings. I mean, honestly, I don't even want wings."

"Look," Ozias said, "I understand that you are frustrated and all but I wouldn't say that around other angels. You would be surprised at how many souls here want wings but could never fill the shoes for the job. I think you can touch the sky."

"Well, how exactly? Ozias, I'm scared of heights!" she huffed. "Is there a way where I can donate mine or something?"

"Uhhh, no," Ozias said flatly, "You're not going to cut them off just because it's not convenient for you. I would probably die if my wings were ripped off of me."

As ironic as that was, Jo tried to keep her chuckle in when she asked. "Why would you *die?*"

"Because that's what makes angels -- well -- angels. Angels are the symbol of peace, and without wings, you're just a wandering soul. It's an important thing that a lot of people don't get to have. If your wings were ripped off of you, you basically are nothing but a wingless angel -- which you wouldn't actually be an angel anymore." Axel wondered if Ozias had ever seen an angel get their wings cut off.

"So what?" Jo replied, "Is that one of your 'All-Time' fears? Having those beautiful white wings ripped off of you?"

"Yes, it is," he replied sincerely, not even shy about it. "I am scared of that. You're scared of heights and Axel is scared of...."

"Psychopaths that are after me," Axel finished for him.

"We all have fears, the angel told her. "So are you going to face them or hide under them?"

Axel saw her thinking about it. Something was going on in that brain of hers that neither Ozias nor Axel knew about when she spoke moments after. "Fine, I'll try again -- on one condition."

"This ought to be something," Axel mumbled.

"What then?" the angel asked, crossing his arms.

"We go see Avy's ballet recital tonight," she replied, crossing her own arms as well.

"Why do you wanna go?" Ozias asked her.

"Well, I promised her that I would go and I'm sure *you* don't want to miss it either," Jo replied, making a singsong voice with the sentence. "So what is it going to be Ozias, the guardian angel of two dead mortals?"

***

"This is insane," Ozias mumbled as they stood in front of the only civic center in town. The center was located downtown right next to the actual ballet conservatory that Avy attended. It was mildly crowded with family and friends coming in to get their seats. "We shouldn't be here."

"Dove Boy," Jo said, "just relax, it's not like anyone will see us."

"It's not the living that I'm worried about," the angel replied.

"Say, do angels worry a lot? Because you, sure enough do," Jo stated.

"So," Axel started, "let me get this straight; Avy is Jo's best friend since middle school and also just so happens to be Ozias' 'little' sister who has no idea that Ozias exists because he was the firstborn miscarriage and she just thinks she's an only child who lost her best friend thanks to her best friend's friend who shot her and now ended up at her ballet recital with her, her best friend's friend who shot her, and her angel brother— and she has no idea they're here?"

"Yeah, sure. We'll go with that," Jo said.

"Does she know that you exist?" Axel asked Ozias.

"How would she know?" Ozias asked. "She doesn't remember."

"Remember what?" Jo asked, confused. Ozias ignored her as he walked towards the multiple double doors to the civic center and the two mortals with wings followed. Up ahead, Jo saw Avy's -- and Ozias' -- parents standing next to her own parents that had decided to go support their daughter's best friend on behalf of Jo. The angel stopped and looked at his relatives with wanting eyes. Of course, his own mother and father didn't glance at him as he watched them interact with Jo's parents. Jo wondered what was going through the angel's head as he saw his own parents interact with hers and not even glancing towards the son they would have had. It was a situation she never expected to have witnessed in her life -- or her death.

But what if Ozias did live? What if he was never a miscarriage and had lived with his family and had been a well-known person? What if he was just a boy and not an angel?

"Ozias," she called. He looked at her then realized he'd watched them for too long. Then without further delay, the angel walked away from them as if he had somewhere else he needed to be -- and of course, the two mortals followed right behind him. Ozias made his way through the people and headed towards the backstage area where they were walking through all the dancers getting ready for their dances. Jo thought this would've been an actual full-on dance production just by how many girls and guys were there getting ready. Making their buns on their heads, reviewing their dance, and spraying their hairspray, made it hard for Jo to breath. Everyone was practically doing the same thing, except for Avy Whitman.

The three of them found the ballerina in her dressing room, sitting on one of the chairs and staring at her reflection in the mirror. She wore this beautiful long silk red skirt that went over her leotard and tights. Her blonde haired bun was surrounded by a red ribbon-like headpiece that was bobby-pinned on her head. The loose end of the ribbon overflowed behind her head and stopped halfway down her back. Looking back and forth at her and Ozias, Jo could now tell they were related. They had the same hair color, same skin tone, same eyes, same facial features but they were worlds apart. One was among the living trying to survive from the society of life. The other had been fighting immortal fights and hoping the living wouldn't leave him and stray.

"What am I doing here?" Avy said to herself quietly as she kept staring down at her reflection.

"You're here to dance," Ozias told her before he sat down on the floor with his legs out and his wings relaxed next to the girl. "You're here to dance for yourself," he said staring at the floor.

"Jo's gone and I'm here preparing myself for a recital," Avy cried.

"She's not entirely gone, Avy," the angel answered.

"I can't do this," Avy thought.

"Yes, you can," Ozias replied in the void. "You've done this so many times."

"But she was supposed to be here," Avy said.

"So was I," he stated.

"Could she hear us?" Axel asked.

Ozias shook his head. "She might if I touch her."

"Touch her?" Jo asked curiously.

Ozias made a warning face at the two. "I've never touched her."

"Why not?" Jo asked confused. "She's your sister. Why haven't you comforted her like you were trying to do now?"

"Because," the angel stated, "you can always scare the living when you try to touch them and do it wrong."

"So you've never touched her because you're scared that you will mess her up?" Axel asked.

"E.J. is the only one that's good at bringing people home. I -- on the other hand -- am not. I mean, look what happened with you two; I tried warning Jo to get away from the soda machine so I could deal with Dezmon but instead, you paid attention to my reflection on the machine and I couldn't stop Dezmon from making Axel kill you. I mean, why do you think it's easy for demons to find victims?"

The two didn't have an answer. But hearing E.J.'s name had brought up questions as to who her "character" really was in the afterlife. Jo had realized Ozias was right. She had paid attention to his reflection and therefore didn't make it out of there alive.

"Because they're good at manipulating the living into being their personal slaves. That's why there are all these bad things in this world. Plane hijackers, the bombing at the Boston Marathon and in Brussels, the

Holocaust, the pimps down the streets selling their prized girl, the over-the-top drinkers, the smokers, gangs and gang leaders, the addiction of drugs, depression, lust, and school shootings. You name it, demons have manipulated it. All of these things were ideas from a demon who gave living people the idea and guess what? The people let them. And this whole mess started with the first angel that fell from Heaven."

"So what part does E.J. play in all of this?" Jo asked randomly. "Is he the fallen angel that started this?"

The angel sighed, "E.J. isn't an angel at all."

"What is he then?"

"He's a person who brings people home," the angel replied. "He's done the job better than any angel ever could if you would just let him take you home."

"What home?" Jo asked.

"Avy, you've got thirty minutes!" hollered a woman who quickly sped down the hallway. Avy rushed to her feet and made her way down the hall while wiping the tears from her eyes. Ozias got up and was half-way out the door when he told the two.

"Home is where E.J. is." The angel disappeared down the hall.

And of course, the two winged mortals followed.

***

"Avy Whitman! You're on deck!" hollered the same woman who had called her from her dressing room. Jo, Axel, and Ozias stood a few feet away from her as they waited from the side curtains of the stage for Ozias' sister's turn.

"She doesn't look good," Jo pointed out. The mortal was right; his sister didn't look like she was ready to dance even though she had been practicing this number for weeks in advance. Ozias knew how many blisters and cuts her feet had from her pointed shoes. He knew how hard it was to stay flexible and continue doing the same routines from class at home. He knew about all of it. Why? Because he had always watched her. Since the day she had drifted away from his gentle grip to go among the living, he had always watched her.

He probably knew more than his own parents would ever know about her but that was the reality when someone's stuck watching from the other side.

"I think you should go talk to her," Jo said, more of a firm statement than a question.

"I can't," he told her, "I don't know how she'll..."

"You're her *brother*," Jo cut in. "You should be able to go comfort her the way a brother should."

"It's not the same," the angel argued, "she wouldn't know who I am and anyways, I've lost that chance of being with her so there's no point in comforting her and letting her down."

"What are you talking about?" Axel burst in.

The angel didn't answer.

"Fine, I'll go since her own brother won't take the risk," Jo said walking towards her. The angel panicked and took the mortal's arm.

"Just because you have wings and can now do the things I do, doesn't mean you know how to use them," he warned her.

"I think I can take care of myself and her, Mr. Perfect," Jo spat and jerked her arm away from his grip. He watched her go up to his sister right when the dancer before her was in the middle part of her dance. Axel stayed quiet, observing the angel and Jo as she went up to Avy. The angel couldn't watch so he focused on the last few moments of the dance that was before Avy's.

"I know you can't hear me," Jo said to Avy. "But I just want you to know that you're not alone in this. Trust me, you've never been alone. I can't imagine what you must be feeling; starting a Monday with your best friend being shot and you now go through that for not only the entire week but for the rest of your life. It's something that's entirely hard to live with. I mean, for about two or three days, I thought this had all been some dream I was in; a dream where my long lost friend Axel came back to town five years later only to have been manipulated by a demon -- who happened to look like one of the four characters I came up with that had no story.

"Then here I am, stuck with seeing everything as if I'm invisible, as if the minute I died, I vanished from everything and everyone. That may be true but it's hard to think there's nothing more to live for since you're not living anymore. You're just stuck in between everything and there's not much way to get out. Then here I get saved by an angel -- I'm not even joking -- and it just so happens to be your older brother who was a miscarriage two years before you came into the world. Yeah, he's good at saving people and fighting demonic psychos but he's still -- in a way -- human. He loves you enough to not comfort you because he's afraid he'll scare you or he'll mess you up.

"He's a protector to you and to everyone else that he seems to care about as well. I guess that's one reason to like your brother." Jo chuckled weakly. "So yeah, I realized this isn't a dream. Sometimes, you think that reality is a dream because of how bad it gets. You wish you could just wake up from it, but you don't wakeup and that's how you know it's real. Maybe we think dreams are better than reality and maybe they are. But why sleep through life when you still have another day ahead of you?"

"Up next is Avy Whitman!" said the voice through the speakers. Ozias saw that Avy started heading towards the stage with...

"Avy," Jo called. With reflex, she took her hand and Avy suddenly stopped looking startled. Ozias couldn't believe what he had just seen. "Don't forget what's real to you." Jo let her go and took a few steps back. Avy looked around as if she thought someone had been there but when she realized that she couldn't find Jo, she made her way to the center of the stage with the confidence that they'd all been waiting to see in her. Jo went up to Ozias as he stared back at her both surprised and disappointed.

"She heard you," he told her in awe. "She really did hear you."

"Maybe she did, maybe she didn't," Jo said. "But maybe she's been waiting to hear a voice like yours to bring her home."

"It's not my place to bring her home." the angel told her. "But I'll admit that I was too scared to do it -- even though I knew I should've done it."

"Maybe one day you will," Axel said, giving him a soft smile as Avy's music was being played in the background. The three of them stopped and stared at the ballerina who danced the night away.

Chapter X

The Burial

A first day somewhere is usually tough for that person no matter where it is. People hope to just make it through the entire day without messing up or being noticed.

Or so sixth grader Jo Silver had thought. Middle school was so unexpected that Jo wished Axel was still there with her. If he were here walking down the hall with her, they both would've been fine. No one would ever dare mess with the two. Because right after word got out they had beat up some boys that were messing with her one day, no one would come near them for almost the entire rest of the school year. But since it was just her, Jo had kept her head down, hoping that no one would bother noticing that she was by herself.

It had only been a few months since Jo saw Axel Lardica driving away down the street for the last time. That day felt longer than when she got home and hid in her room thinking the whole time he was really gone. It had been like that for most of the summer. Of course, they had emailed each other many times a day, telling each other what was going on throughout the day or week. Jo didn't realize it until it was too late but little by little, Axel was fading away.

It started with a few days when he didn't email her back. Luckily, he replied on the weekend saying things got crazy and he didn't have time to respond. Jo didn't mind because she had thought that it would occasionally happen. But then he stopped responding for about two weeks straight. Jo had been emailing him to see if he was okay but he didn't reply for another few days more. Weeks turned into a month and that was when Jo knew something was wrong. She had kept emailing and emailing hoping one day he would respond.

But he never did.

The last thing Axel had emailed Jo was: *I wish I was home.* She always would go back to that email and stare at those five words that were from him for hours. There had been a time when she thought if she stared at it so hard and concentrated on it, he would say something again and things went back to the way they were. Jo had given up on that hopeless dream on the first day of middle school. She had to accept he had drifted away and was never going to come back. She had to move on from it.

Jo thought her first day of middle school would make things worse. At first, it kinda did when she ran into someone in the hallway because she wasn't looking where she was going. All of her stuff -- and the stuff from the person she clashed into -- landed on the floor and everything was everywhere.

"I'm so sorry. I didn't see you there and..." Jo went on as she quickly tried to pick up her stuff without the chance of seeing who she had run into.

"No, you're fine. It's okay trust me! WAIT!" It was a girl who had gasped, and she had picked up one of Jo's books holding it in her hands after she had grabbed all of her things. "I LOVE THIS BOOK!!!" she exclaimed excitedly when she stood up.

Jo was surprised. *"Really?"* The girl held Jo's copy of *Inkheart* her grandma had bought her at the bookstore. For Jo, she had seen the movie when she was very young when it had first come out, but it had never occurred to her until recently that it was actually based off of a book -- a trilogy to be more specific. The girl's blonde hair was pulled back in a tight slick bun. She wore leggings with a long shirt and soft boots. She looked like she could've been a dancer or something that involved the theater.

"Yes! Oh my, I totally ship Meggie and Farid! I think they are so cute together and I've been longing to find someone -- just anyone -- that has read it because no one had and then I found you with it and I'm just..." she went on and on about how great the trilogy was and Jo didn't mind the girl talking about it so much because it meant a lot to Jo that she found someone like herself.

"Yeah, I just started this and will eventually get into the other two books," Jo told her.

"You should!" the girl encouraged. "I mean, I wish they made movies for the other two books because they're so good and I love them so much!"

"Yeah, me too!" Jo agreed.

"I didn't catch your name," the girl said.

"I go by Jo," she said, extending her hand out. "Jo Silver."

"Avy Whitman," she said, taking Jo's hand.

***

"It's Saturday," Jo said after waking up in the shed that was in her backyard.

"Naw," came Axel, "It's Monday." The black stains on his neck and wrists were now faded, which made Jo happy.

"Very funny," Jo playfully shoved him from where he was sitting.

"Ah, ya wanna play that game?" Axel challenged, then he jumped on her and starting to pin her down when she gave an enormous flap of her wings, making Axel go off balance and he fell off of her. She then got on top of him and pinned him down.

"Might I remind you who taught me to fight back?"

"Wait, let me guess," Axel said, then in a flash she let her guard down, shoved her off of him and rolled right on top again. "Me?"

"You forgot someone," Jo corrected him, slapping him off with her wings and standing up immediately before he could jump on her again. "Ozias did too."

"He doesn't count," Axel protested.

"Why not?" Jo asked.

"Because he's an angel."

"So are we."

"No, we're not. We're..."

"Mortals with wings," both said in unison, mimicking Ozias' voice. The angel kept trying to explain to them that they are NOT angels so therefore, they are mortals who just so happen to have wings.

"You guys can't give an angel a few minutes more sleep?" grumbled Ozias from the floor. He opened one of his wings that was covering his face and most of his body from the morning sun. "I mean, it's not like you're both cats and are good at fighting quietly."

"Aww, is sleepy head in a bad mood today?" Jo asked as if she was talking to a baby. Ozias put his wing back over him, indicating he was still attempting to sleep some more. He mumbled something about mortals acting like five-year-olds who don't know how to be quiet during "nap time."

"Hey!" Axel jumped in, "You're technically a mortal with wings too."

"Says who?" muffled Ozias.

"Says you, that's who," Axel replied.

"Can I just have a few minutes of sleep to myself?" pleaded the angel. "I seriously got more sleep when you two were among the living than now."

"Speaking of life, my funeral's today," Jo mentioned as if it was an everyday thing.

"Good for you," groaned Ozias. "I never got a funeral."

"Complaining much?"

"What do you two want from me?" the angel asked.

"We want to go to the funeral."

Ozias' wings opened again but with much more speed than the first time before. "You're joking, right?"

"No, we want to go," Axel said. "Don't dead people get to go to their own funeral?"

"No, because they would already be in their eternal home by now and not stuck here," Ozias explained, grudgingly getting up from his sleeping position. "I don't think it's a good idea to go. I've already broken a lot of rules for you two and I think it'll be too dangerous to go."

"Danger? Danger's my middle name," Jo said, cocking her head upward.

"Annabel is your middle name," Ozias said flatly.

"Why have you gotta know everything?" she exclaimed.

"Because I'm.."

"An *angel*," both Axel and Jo said in unison.

"What did you two take this morning?" Ozias thought out loud. "But seriously, I wasn't letting you go anyway because we have to go."

"Where are we going that's so important?" whined Jo.

"I was going to take you to see E.J. Maybe he can help us on this."

"WHAT?!?!" both mortals exclaimed.

"But you know, you guys want to go to some funeral," Ozias said as if he didn't care.

"Why don't we compromise this?" Jo suggested, "We go to the funeral and right after go see E.J. -- wherever he is."

"Uh, no," the angel argued. "We are not going to the funeral."

"Let's vote then," Axel joined in.

"We are not...."

"All in favor of doing both things, say I," Axel said with his hand leveled up to his head. "I,"

"I," Jo said as well.

"This isn't a debate," Ozias said, crossing his arms. "We're not going and that's final!" He sounded like a dad saying to his two teenagers they couldn't go to the concert.

"Well, too bad because you can't keep us from going," Jo said, crossing her arms. "We're not leaving until after we go to that funeral whether you like it or not."

***

"We finally made it," Jo said as the three stood at the building where the ceremony was held. She saw many familiar people, all wearing black, passing by them to get inside. It was strange to think she was attending her own funeral, but she knew she wanted to go. She wasn't exactly sure why since it was already hard enough for her to watch from this side of things, but something told her she couldn't miss it.

"As soon as it's over, we're heading out," Ozias said, nervously scanning the crowd.

"What?" Axel said, looking at him. "You're scared of going to a funeral ceremony?"

"No," the angel replied, "It's not the ceremony that I'm worried about. I just have a bad feeling about this."

"Oh, give me a break," Jo said, already walking towards the entrance. "We're going to be fine." The three entered at the same time, passing by -- and through -- people as they made their way to the main room. On top of the stage was a podium on the far left with a microphone curved on the top. From there she saw two good size coffins that were parallel to each other with two big pictures that were right beside them. The picture on the left was of her, and the picture on the right was of Axel.

"Why is my picture up there?" Axel asked. "Isn't this supposed to be Jo's funeral?"

"Well," the angel replied. "I forgot to mention that Jo's parents were willing to share Jo's funeral with you since you two had a history together."

"But aren't they..." Axel didn't finish his sentence because something else had caught his eye. There walking up the stairs of the stage to Axel's coffin was a woman who wore a long black dress with flat shoes. It didn't show much of her from behind, but Axel knew exactly who she was.

Hurriedly, Axel went down the aisle towards the stage and stopped when he was a few feet away from the woman who was next to his coffin. "Mom?" he called to her weakly with water filling his eyes.

She didn't respond. Instead, she just stared at her son -- her son in the coffin with his eyes closed, dressed in a nice suit. The only thing they both had in common was the black bandana Jo had given him that was still on his left wrist. Slowly, he took a few steps closer until he was next to her, staring at himself in the coffin. His wings felt heavier as he felt the void in the atmosphere around them.

"I'm sorry, Mom," he said, with his voice cracking. "I'm so sorry for leaving you. I didn't mean to.."

"I know you're not here," Axel's mother said softly. "I know you are probably in a better place than here in this coffin. But if you can hear this -- if you can hear me -- please listen." She paused, still looking down at her son in the coffin. "I wish I knew why you did it -- why you shot one of your good friends before killing yourself -- but sometimes I get the feeling that I already know why. It's my fault -- in a way -- that I took you from the things you knew at home because your father was there. I was just wanting to start fresh and I had to do it with him out of the picture. But instead, I brought you into the mess I made, bringing home Marshall -- believing he was a good dad figure for you.

"But I was wrong again," she said, her voice cracking as tears streamed down her face.

"Mom, it's okay," Axel said soothingly. "Please don't blame yourself for this. It was all me."

"The last time I saw you was when you fought against Marshall. You had bruises all over your face and I couldn't help but think that this was all because of me wanting a second chance at life and love.

"Sometimes the things we want will affect other people in a way we never intended them to happen." Axel's mother dug into her purse and pulled out a piece of paper that was folded nicely in her hands. He recognized his handwriting on it as she tucked the paper in the palm of her son in the coffin. It was the note he left her before he had set off from Texas, the note he carefully wrote out to her moments before his departure because there was no way he could've described everything he thought on that small slip of paper.

I'm sorry for leaving you but I have to find my second chance.

– Axel

—was what he wrote on the paper that was now in his hands in the coffin.

"I hope you found your second chance," his mother told him, blowing a gentle kiss towards her son in the coffin. Before she walked away, Axel took her right hand into his left hand -- feeling her gentle skin for the first time in a while. She stopped and stared down not at her hand, but what was holding it.

"I love you, Mom," he whispered in her ear. "I love you so much." Softly, he let her go and turned his back on her and walked away towards....

"I love you too, Axel."

Axel stopped. He glanced back to see his mother glancing out away from the coffin as if she was looking for him towards the audience.

Axel's mother had heard his voice from the other side. A tear streamed down his smiling face as he turned back around and kept walking. He was hugged by both Jo and Ozias before he even made it halfway down the aisle that stood in the middle of rows and rows of chairs. He didn't care about the tears that kept streaming down his face for in that moment, he regretted the second chance he took for granted. Hearing his own mother talk to him made him ask himself why he didn't fight harder against Dezmon's chains?

Maybe, he had thought, it was because he wasn't strong enough to push him back. Maybe -- like Ozias had said before -- he had just let the demon do what he wanted. Maybe he deserved to have this happen -- he deserved to watch his mother cry for her dead, selfish, suicidal son that was lost in the world he was in. He deserved to be chained up somewhere in Hell with Dezmon right there torturing him. But Jo shouldn't watch her own funeral take place. She should've been sitting with her parents, wondering to herself what had happened to the real Axel Lardica instead of being dead with him. She shouldn't...

"Don't think like that," Ozias whispered in his ear. The angel had heard his thoughts. "Don't beat yourself up so hard about this."

"But I do deserve it," he sobbed.

"Look at me," Jo demanded. He found her tear stained face looking back at his. "Honestly, I'd rather be dead with you knowing why you did what you did than to find out that you're gone and me never knowing what happened to my best friend, Axel Lardica. Okay? So what if we're gone for eternity? This is all we have and we have to push through it like we're still living. We have to make this second chance worth it. I mean look at us; we're mortals who have wings! And I'm scared of heights! But hey! Maybe in this life, I won't be anymore."

"That's interesting," came Ozias jokingly, "because yesterday you were still scared of heights." After Jo told Ozias to shut up, all three of them burst into laughter amongst the dried tears.

"We're stuck with each other and I don't mind," Jo said.

"Me too," Axel agreed.

"C'mon you too," the angel said, "we have to get seats or something. Service is about to start."

Although they were in ghost-like forms and could've found a spot in the front row, they still sat in the back where there was an entire empty row for the three of them to sit in. The service started with a pastor that had baptized her when she was younger -- before her family stopped attending church -- talking about all the things that made Jo, well, Jo. He went on about all the things that he wouldn't really know unless her parents had told him things about her for this ceremony.

Then the pastor started talking about her friendship with Axel and how the two were neighbors and had been friends since she had moved into town when she was younger -- talking about all the adventures the two had before Axel moved to Texas. He talked about Axel as if he knew him his whole life -- but of course, he didn't.

That was when he announced that Avy was doing *both* Jo and Axel's eulogies for the service. Shocking to the two mortals, but they noticed that Ozias wasn't surprised at all. In fact, he looked rather nervous during the entire thing. He kept scanning the doors while bouncing his leg up and down.

"How long have you known all these details?" Jo whispered to him, even though it wasn't necessary since no one could hear them anyway.

"You guys were out for two days while you grew those wings," he replied, sounding nervous. "What was I supposed to do? Stand around and watch wings for the millionth time grow out? I always get around to finding things out."

"What are you nervous about?" Axel asked, catching the angel's vibe.

"Huh?"

"Your leg's bouncing and you keep looking around the place," Jo explained.

"It just doesn't feel safe here."

"Again with the 'gut feeling' froyo?" Jo asked annoyed. "Just relax for once, okay? We're not going to get eaten by lions."

"Interesting reference, but it's not the lions that I'm concerned about."

"Well, quit thinking that everything could go wrong when it won't," Jo said.

Avy started reading from a piece of paper behind the podium that had her written eulogy for the two of them. She told the audience about the first day Jo and Avy met on the first day of middle school where they clashed with each other and Avy saw Jo's copy of *Inkheart*. "I was so happy to have found her with that book because no one I knew read it and it was cool to find someone that actually did."

She went on about how the two had become fan girls throughout the years; fan girls of anything they saw or heard. "It really became an addiction. Watching things like The Breakfast Club and catching up on Once Upon A Time was what made us more open to exploring new genres of books, movies, and songs. We couldn't stop finding more things to be fans of and really, we didn't care how crazy we got when we came up with plot twists and theories for them."

"Jo never really told me much about herself before we became friends and I just found out why. I don't know much about Axel, but I believe that maybe he might've been as close to Jo as I was. I mean, hearing about their adventures from both their parents made me try to imagine what they were like as kids.

"What I don't get is how in the world did they both end up dead during Monday's lunch break at school? I mean yeah, Axel shot her, then himself, but there was more to it than what the school saw. I didn't realize that because I cried so much this whole week for Jo. I had anger towards Axel," she paused, taking a deep breath. Jo felt Axel tensing up when she said that.

"I was mad at him for taking my best friend's life away from her. I was mad that he kept saying he was sorry to Jo moments before he pulled the trigger and I screamed on the inside 'then don't do it!', but he still did. I was mad he did all of it without a proper explanation. What did he mean by wanting a second chance? Isn't that supposed to be while you're still alive?

"You see, I jumped to conclusions without knowing the entire story. I didn't really know that he was friends with Jo before she became friends with me. I had no idea his parents split up and he had to move to Texas. I had no idea what it must've been like for him to not find a home there. I was told he had to fight his way through everything and always came home with a bruised face and bloody knuckles. He was struggling with life probably more than we all thought he was because he wouldn't tell anyone. Why? Because it shows weakness when we confess.

"I assume that eventually, he couldn't just think about it. He had to find a second chance of his own. It was probably driving him crazy not being able to do anything about it. For him, maybe a second chance meant dying here and finding it in the afterlife or whatever happens after you stop living. But he didn't want to go alone. Axel wanted to be on his journey with the person that probably was the closest thing to home there was for him -- and it was the one and only Jo Silver.

"Needless to say, I think we've all gone through a time where we think our first chance has ended for us and we're in search for the second one to come around the corner. We're trying to find the second chance to tell a story or find home again and we don't see that second chances are another set of choices we make in this life.

"I do hope that Jo finds a story to tell wherever she is at this point. And I wish Axel good luck in finding his way back home again and finding the new set of choices for his own second chance. Just as Twenty One Pilots sings in Goner, 'Don't let me be gone,' let us not have them be gone from us. Thank you." The audience applauded as she went down the steps and made her way back to her seat. The service ended with everyone singing *Amazing Grace* as one and they were all dismissed to go to the reception.

"Well, it wouldn't hurt to go to the reception," Jo said sweetly. "It is a part of the service."

"Yeah," Axel agreed, looking at Ozias. But the angel was too busy looking elsewhere that he didn't pay attention to the two mortals until he glanced back at them.

"Oh, sorry," the angel said. "What did you say?"

"Stop," Jo told him, "Stop it right now."

"What?" he asked, confused.

"You're acting like 'the afterlife is under attack and we have to hide everywhere to avoid it,'" she replied dramatically.

"You can't make me ignore my gut feeling if I know it's right," the angel told them both. "I honestly think it still isn't a good idea to be here." Jo stopped in her path walking out of the big sanctuary and turned to face him.

"Why can't we just do things that don't involve your stupid worrying about everything?" Jo exclaimed at him. "You always ruin moments because you're worried that stupid things are going to happen! Well, stop! Quit worrying about every little thing and just let us enjoy this!" Axel said nothing, but it seemed like he was siding with her.

The angel looked at them in disbelief with them against him. "Fine," he said calmly, not even a hint of fury in his voice. "Go and do what you mortals want to do." The angel turned around and started walking away from them.

"Fine!" Jo hollered back, "Enjoy your little pity party!"

The angel kept walking away, not ever saying another word to them as his gut still stirred with worry.

Chapter XI

Sacrifice

The reception was held in another room smaller than the sanctuary but still big enough to fit everyone that attended. Axel had not expected anyone to show up for him--let alone have his own funeral with Jo's.

Jo walked into the crowd with confidence and enjoyment though Axel wasn't sure about expressing the same in that moment. Maybe Ozias was right and something weird was going on that neither Jo nor Axel knew about.

It was not even ten minutes into the reception that he realized Ozias wasn't in there with them. "Jo."

"Yeah?" she asked, turning to face him.

"Ozias isn't here."

"Who cares anymore, if Ozias didn't do his job to watch us or not?" she asked with no sympathy. "He's probably complaining about us in some sacred church on one of his daily prayers with his own beliefs. Give me a break."

"You shouldn't have fought with him like that," Axel told her. "What if he's right? What if demons show up or something much worse comes around?"

"Now you're acting like a true angel, huh?" she said, cutting through with sarcasm. "If you're so worried about him, why don't you go check to see if he's okay yourself?"

"Okay, I will then," Axel said, walking away from her and out of the crowd. He went back to the sanctuary to see if the angel was still there. No one was there except for the two closed coffins on the stage.

Everything was dead silent. Maybe the angel was outside taking time to calm down, Axel thought. Leaving the room, he made his way through the doors that led outside. The mortal scanned the parking lot to see if he...

He found the glowing white wings near the grassy area where it forms into fields of gravestones surrounding the building. The angel looked out of breath and was doing his best to keep his fists up covering his face as a swarm of dark figures with chains in their hands surrounded him in a circle with Dezmon among them. Avy was there too, sitting on the curb with her back against it all while looking out beyond the parking lot – not even noticing that her angel brother was in danger.

"You are too sacrificial," Dezmon told Ozias. "You would rather fight for everyone else -- whether they care about you or not -- than ever fighting for yourself."

Ozias said nothing as he looked at all the demons that were there, waiting to take hold of whatever angel fight he had left in him.

"You want to be just like E.J. right?" Dezmon asked. "You want to do all the 'love thy neighbor' crap and the sinless act and be good at bringing people home, right? He's your role model and you would hate to fail him for not keeping those two mortals with you alive -- or dead."

Ozias stood there, still not saying a single word.

"Well, I have a role model too, ya know," Dezmon told him, not waiting for an answer. "It's pretty obvious who it is, am I wrong?"

"What do you want?" Ozias asked.

"I want you to choose these two options," Dezmon started, "You have the choice of giving me those two winged mortals and you can walk away without any blood on you, or you can decide to be all angel-like and say no, then find out in the end what will happen to you."

"You think I would betray them just like that?" Ozias asked. "You already know my answer, Dezmon. Now get on with it."

"So be it," Dezmon replied with a demonic smirk on his face. Axel panicked as all the demons attacked Ozias, giving him no chance to escape. The chains rattled and clanged with the demon screeches as they covered the angel to where all Axel could see was the demons over him and Dezmon just standing there watching. The boy rushed back into the building and sped through the crowd to the reception room and found Jo, took hold of her arm, and dragged her out of there.

"What the heck are you doing?" she exclaimed, trying to resist.

"Dezmon and a bunch of demons are attacking Ozias as we speak!" he said quickly, making it out the door with her.

"*What?*" she said in shock.

"He was right, Jo!" Axel yelled back at her as they found the sun. Looking over, Axel saw that the demons had surrounded Ozias again but this time, the demons were holding the extremely long chains that were attached to the white angel. The angel was chained around his neck, his wrists, and his ankles. Even his wings were chained together so he wouldn't be able to fly away.

"Oh no..." Jo said as they saw that the demons had opened up a portal to their underworld. Ozias was crawling towards Avy because the chains were too heavy for him to walk to her.

"You should've let her know how much you loved her before all of this happened," Dezmon told the angel. "Because you won't be able to see her again." Then he went airborne and dove into the portal as the other demons followed, bringing the chains down with all of them.

"Ozias!" Jo cried as the two sped towards him. He was halfway to touching Avy but the long chain was getting shorter as the other end was being pulled down. Jo took ahold of one hand as Axel took the other, attempting to pull him closer to Avy and away from the portal but the angel resisted the two mortals.

"I'm sorry! I should've listened to you and I should've known you were right..." Jo said, freaking out.

"Listen to me!" the angel yelled at them. "Whatever you do, do not come find me! Do you understand?"

"What? Are you *crazy?*" Axel questioned, still trying to pull Ozias.

"I mean it!" Ozias cried out. "Do not plan to come rescue me! Go find E.J.!"

"We're not letting you go down there..."

"I'M SERIOUS!" he yelled at them before he was suddenly jerked back quickly towards the portal. The two ran up to try and stop him from going to the underworld, but he was being pulled faster than they could keep up.

"OZIAS!" Axel cried.

"I'M SORRY!" Jo exclaimed.

"DO NOT GO TO HELL!" was all the angel said before he was swallowed up by darkness and the portal closed after he went in. Jo fell on her knees right where the portal had been and cried while apologizing to him. Axel held her in his arms in fear as he glanced at Avy who had sat there the whole time and didn't notice the disappearance of her brother.

"He's gone," Axel whispered to himself in horror. "Ozias is gone."

"And it's all our fault!" wept Jo. "It's all our fault that he's now in Hell."

"What have we done?" Axel asked among the void because it was truly their doing that sent an angel to Hell.

***

He was only about four months into the process before he was to go into the other world he had been watching for so long. He couldn't wait for the day when he went to be with his family without the barrier of the other side.

"Just a few months left," he said in joy as he walked down the street with his parents, heading towards the ice cream shop that was downtown. Entering the place, he seemed in awe at all the things this new world had to offer. The ice cream shop was also a mini store that offered rustic décor and gift ideas for people. They sold regular food such as the hot dog things and the thing they call hamburger -- even though there's no actual ham in it. His parents both ordered cookies and cream flavored ice cream and sat down at one of the tables to enjoy it.

As they did, he decided to walk around the store and get to know what all the things were called since he hadn't had a chance to in a while.

Popsicles, chocolate bars, tea, signs, bags... he practiced, running through all the things he knew in his head as the bell rang indicating that someone had come into the store. He looked over to find a girl about sixteen walking in with a boy who was around his age trailing behind. Both the girl and the boy had similarities but yet the boy had some different features to him. He looked nervous and lost as the two entered in. He decided to continue exploring the new stuff as the girl went to get ice cream. She didn't seem too well and looked rather nauseous as she paid the cashier for her giant sundae.

The boy that came in with her was gone and he couldn't see where he had went. She didn't seem to notice that he wasn't there. Turning around to go towards the ice cream shop's door, he somehow ran into a figure making him lose his balance and fell.

Wait a minute. He *never* runs into anything. Sitting up, he was faced with the boy that walked in with the girl. He was startled to find the boy staring back at him which could only mean one thing.

"You can see me?" he asked the boy.

"Y-Yeah," the boy replied nervously. "You see me?"

"Yeah," he replied. "Are you waiting for your due date?"

"My what?" the boy said, confused. If he didn't know about his due date then he must be new or something. Did anyone from Heaven come down to tell him the details yet? Probably not since the boy seemed to have no clue as to what was going on.

"How long have you been around here?" he asked the boy.

"A few days," the boy replied, looking around him as if he had never seen any of the stuff in the store.

"There hasn't been an angel with you, has there?" he asked.

"N-No," was all the boy said.

"Who are your parents?" he asked the boy.

The boy pointed at the girl who sat by herself on one of the tables outside.

"Oh," was all he could really think to say. "Umm, so what do you know?"

The boy hesitated as if he was trying to decide whether to trust him or not. "I've been here for a few days following her and haven't seen anyone like me until I saw you. I don't think she knows I'm here," he said, referring to the sixteen-year-old.

"It takes awhile for them to realize we're here," he told the boy. "So I assume you don't have a name yet."

"No," the boy replied. "Do you?"

He pointed at his parents who were a few feet away from them. "They are leaning towards the name Ozias. It would probably be Ozias Whitman."

"I guess Ozias does suit you," the boy said. "Got any ideas for my name?"

Ozias looked at him carefully as if the name was written on his forehead. His hair was darker than any hair he had ever seen. His skin was paler than white and he looked similar to the boy that went into the lion's den and made it out alive because God sent angels down to shut the lion's mouths.

"Does Daniel suit you?" Ozias offered.

"I guess we'll eventually find out," Daniel replied, smiling at his new friend.

***

Walking down the pathway the walls became dark metal bars, and he could still hear the screams from the thousands of souls begging the demons for something. Some want just one drop of cool water. Others plead for their flesh to stop burning. Some even wish for E.J. to come down and save them from their eternity in Hell. But it's not the demons' job to grant any of their wishes. They chose where they wanted to go and that's what they got.

He stopped at one of the cell doors and opened it up. "Get up," he snapped.

The angel said nothing as he slowly got to his feet. He took hold of the chain line that was connected to his neck and pulled on it for fun. His hands were chained together and so were his feet, but he could still walk by himself. His wings were wrapped in chains in a way where he couldn't fly if he tried. He unhooked the prisoner from the chains that were attached to the walls and kept a good grip on the chain link that was attached to the angel's neck. Then he led him back down the hall where he had come from, heading towards the main building.

"Is this really your dream come true?" the angel asked him. "Bonding me in chains pulling me around like a dog on a leash?"

"Why wouldn't it be?" the demon grinned. "It's all I ever wanted."

"And what about us being guardian angels?" the angel asked. "What about that dream?"

"I wanted no part of helping mortals get through their pathetic tough times," the demon replied, spitting at the angel's face. "You forced me into it."

"Is it because of your mom?"

"Why are you asking me questions *you* already know?" the demon roared.

"Because I care to hear them from you," the angel replied. "You know how much you mean to me."

"Yeah," the demon said, "all I am to you now is a demon."

"Why do you think I said that?" the angel asked him. "Because I can't find who you were before your wings went dark."

"You're just trying to save yourself from whatever we have in store for you." the demon said flatly. "That's all this really is at this point."

"Daniel," Ozias called.

The demon stopped in his tracks, with his face turning red with fury. His hands curled into a fist so tightly, his fingernails were digging into his palm. In a flash, the demon turned around and slapped the angel so hard, he stumbled to the ground. In the process he scratched his face with his nails. "WHY ARE CALLING ME BY THAT NAME?" the demon boomed at his face.

The angel slowly sat up and looked at the demon as tiny red lines of blood formed on his face. "An old friend gave you that name when you had none," he said calmly with some sadness that had formed in his voice.

The demon stared at him because there were no other words he could find to say. They'd been enemies more years than they ever were friends, fighting against each other about the same mortals who had stood next to him since they had died. Why? Oh, because he was an angel and people would always go for the angels after seeing a demon. But it was not the angel's place to take the two into his hands and keep them from their eternity. The demon's job was to bring them back to Hell and finish the plan, not have the angel come and take over and end up fighting more for them than ever.

The angel broke the rules, and yet his wings were still as white as snow as if he was always perfect. Perfect to ruin the demon's job and get him in trouble for not bringing the two dead souls back. He claimed to be an old friend. "You never really were one," the demon said, turning around and continuing to drag the angel to the King of Hell.

They made it to an enormous throne room that was lit up by torches for light. Pillars stood side by side on both the left and right of the place as they went down the middle. On them were red and black paintings of demons surrounding the living, doing things that demons forced them to do in order to win. The demon didn't look back at the angel for his eyes were on the King of Hell himself.

There he sat on his throne, wings outstretched and relaxed behind him. His skin was as gray as smoke and his head was scarred with burns that looked like it happened years ago -- the reason why he didn't have hair on his head. He wore all black like everyone else -- including black Converse -- but when you took a good look at him, he appeared to be only be a few years older than both the demon and the angel. Next to him were two humans in chains, both with brown hair wearing all black. One was male and one was female.

At the foot of his throne, the demon bowed to him and didn't come back up until he was told to. "So this is the angel that broke the rules?" he came, sounding interested.

"Yes, it is," the demon confirmed. "I was able to get him at both of the mortals' funeral they attended."

"Interesting," the king said. The angel said nothing to either of them. He just stood there and watched as they talked about him in his presence. "Surely you're proud that you brought him in chains just as I had requested."

"Indeed, I am," the demon replied.

"Speak your name," commanded the king to the angel.

"Ozias Whitman," the angel replied, doing his best to inhale and exhale. The demon knew that it was scary enough being in Hell. But what made it horrifying was when an angel found himself in the hands of Abaddon himself.

"Whitman? As for the last name?" the king repeated.

"He's an Unborn Angel," the demon explained.

"How fascinating this situation is," the king admitted. "Him as an Unborn Angel and you as an Unwished-For *Fallen* Angel. I wonder how you two had ever become friends in the first place. You both seem polar opposites from each other now."

The demon looked at the angel wondering to himself why he ever bothered being friends with this angel that he held as a prisoner. The same one that he ran into at that ice cream shop. The one that gave him a name when he had none. The one that had been there with the demon as the demon watched his own mother take away his life from him. The same person that had come up with the great idea of becoming angels. The one and only Ozias Whitman that pushed him off of Heaven when his wings got dark -- when things didn't end the way they had imagined.

"He's nothing more than an enemy to me," the demon assured Abaddon as his eyes were met by the angel's blue ones. The angel looked at the demon with sorrow when he told him that. As if he wasn't the one that pushed him off.

The demon looked back at the king. "Now, have I gained your trust that you have offered me in order to become your own second-in-command?"

The king looked at the chained angel, then back at the demon and smiled demonically. "There is just one thing left I must challenge you with," he said finally.

"Anything for the King of Hell," the demon acknowledged.

"Every demon that exists will go through the same test I am giving you now at some point in this afterlife," the demon king started, "It truly shows the true colors of what you really have in you."

"Tell me what I shall do," the demon urged.

The king signaled one of the other demons that were in the room. The other demon went up to him with a giant machete in his hands and gave it to the king. Abaddon rose from his throne and walked towards the demon. He stopped right in front of the demon and handed him the machete in his hands. "Remove the angel's wings."

Dezmon stood there, not sure if he heard right from Abaddon. "Sir?"

"Remove the angel's wings," Abaddon repeated. "Tie him to one of these pillars and cut his wings off of him. You say he's only an enemy to you. Now show me that he is," the king said, crossing his arms as his wings relaxed behind him.

Dezmon turned to face the angel who turned as pale as his skin while other demons used small daggers to rip his white shirt off of him -- making his chest bare. He'd always wanted to remove angel's wings but he'd never thought it would be Ozias' wings. It would've been easier if he didn't know who the angel was he was to rip the wings off of because in that moment -- looking at Ozias -- he almost thought he couldn't do it. He was close enough to say no to it. But Dezmon then looked away from the blue eyes as he led the angel to one of the side pillars that was closer to them. He used the long chain link that was around the angel's neck and wrapped it tightly around the pillar along with Ozias' body and left his chained wings free.

"An enemy is all he is to you." Abaddon quoted from behind him.

The demon's hand that was holding the machete was shaking violently as he met the blue eyes again. It was obvious that Ozias was scared of not how much it was going to hurt but how much more pain he would have from not being an angel anymore. The angel was on the verge of tears as Dezmon walked closer to him.

The demon took hold of the humerus part of both angel's wings with his right hand and had the machete in the other. He tried to breathe thoroughly, hoping that his shaking hand would stop vibrating. "I'm sorry," he said quietly.

Tears were rushing down Ozias' face as he shut his eyes tightly. "You're still going to find the light back home."

At that moment, Dezmon knew he shouldn't do it. It felt wrong to do this to Ozias. Deep down inside, Dezmon knew that Ozias had no other choice but to push him off of Heaven. He knew this was all fake. None of this was real anymore. He should just ignore Abaddon's orders and take the blame he was meant to have. But instead, the demon's mouth got close to the angel's ear as he whispered softly. "One day, you'll fly again."

Dezmon tried his best to ignore Ozias' screams as blood was everywhere. The demon tried to finish the job as quickly as possible, making every swing count so that it would end soon. So that Ozias' tears would stop streaming down his face, and his bloody screams would end as well. But even after Ozias' wings fell to the floor behind the angel, Ozias still cried in pain for what felt like a thousand years.

Deep down inside Dezmon knew that one day, Ozias would fly again.

Just not today.

Chapter XII

Life of the Party

"Jo?" Axel whispered weakly, still having his arms around her.

"Y-Yeah?" she croaked, still stuck in the same position she had been in for the past few hours. The reception was over and it had been two or three hours since they saw Ozias vanish into the black portal to Hell. Everyone that had been there were now gone, carrying on with their lives while the two dead mortals sat on the grass where the ambush had been held and mourn for the angel that was no longer with them in this cruel afterlife. Even Avy had walked away moments after the disappearance of her angel brother as if she hadn't even seen all that happening.

But that was the thing: the living couldn't see what was going on in the afterlife. And it made Jo wonder what other things had she missed when she was still alive.

"I think..." Axel said hesitantly, "that we should go find this E.J."

Surprised as she was, she sat up to look into his hazel eyes. "Go find him?"

"Y-Yeah," he said. "maybe he could help us get Ozias back."

"But how would we find him?" Jo asked. "We don't even know who he is here."

"Wouldn't you know?" he asked her. "You're the one who made them all up, right?"

"Oh so it's *my* fault that this happened," she said expressively.

"No, I didn't say that," Axel said, trying not to sound too defensive.

"THEN WHAT ARE YOU TRYING TO SAY?" Jo screamed. Axel flinched and reflected the same face he had when she yelled at him in the janitor's closet back at the school. She didn't want to go back to that type of situation again with him. "I'm sorry," she whispered.

"It's okay," Axel said assuredly. "You're just scared, that's all."

He wasn't wrong. She was scared. She was scared that there would be no way to fix anything in this new "life" again. Scared that it was her fault for not listening to Ozias when he had those true gut feelings about demons lurking by. Scared of what would happen to him down there. And even more scared of what would happen to both her and Axel without him. "Why did I ever think up these guys?" she mumbled to herself.

"What?"

"You know, my um, characters," she explained. "Ozias and Dezmon look so much how I had pictured them but yet, they're so far from what I thought they would ever be. I mean, I never thought I would find two of my characters having wings and fighting with each other constantly. And now I'm scared to find out who the real E.J. and Abaddon are here. It makes me realize that I basically wanted to write a stupid story with some people that live up to be greater than a stupid story that a teenage mortal wanted to write.

"And I thought about what their story really is versus the one I wanted to come up with. I wouldn't even know that they didn't exist with an untold story to tell if I was still alive," she said.

"What if you were still alive and you knew their story?" Axel asked.

"But I'm not..."

"What if you were," he said. "What would you do?"

"Well," she started, thinking thoroughly about this. "I would tell their story. I would tell it the way it all happened and find a way to make it seem so accurate that when people got to the afterlife, they would realize that all of it is true about the Unborn Angel fighting against the Unwished-For Angel. About life isn't the same as death. And about how to live through it."

"What about us?" he asked. "Would you write about the boy who shot the girl with no story only to find his second chance?"

"I guess I would," she replied. "We are in a way, tied up in this story too."

"Okay," he stopped and had a thinking expression on his face before he spoke again. "But shouldn't we finish the story and try to figure this out?"

"Yeah," she agreed. "But I think it's up to us to get Ozias back. There's no time in finding E.J. and I don't think Ozias has any time left."

"So do you have a plan then, Jo Silver?" Axel asked her.

"Yeah," she replied looking out towards the sun as it was almost dusk. "I think I do."

***

"You sure about this?" Axel asked worriedly.

"We have to do it," Jo answered him. "We have to get Ozias back." In order for Jo's plan to work, the two had to find a place where they knew for sure that a demon would be present -- at a random teenager's party. They found one in one of the few cookie-cutter subdivisions in town. It was pretty easy spotting the multiple cars parked in the same area with teenagers everywhere and music blasting the closer they got. All they really had to do was find any nearby demon, capture him, and force him to open a portal to Hell. It all seemed like a piece of cake but really, it wasn't.

"Let's go crash a mortal's party then," Axel said encouragingly.

And so they did. But it wasn't much for them to crash the party since no one knew they were crashing the party because they were invisible to all the living. Axel noticed as they walked through the door -- literally -- that the attendance of the party basically had the rich teenagers making a dent in their parents' beer and wine. It was, in fact, a madhouse with not only the music blasting but people with slurred words and wobbly legs and food everywhere. Axel had never been to a school party such as this but he, sure enough, didn't care for going to one ever in his whole afterlife again.

It was just a stupid thing to do. He would see some teens flirting with each other, some would drink endlessly until everything inside of them was spinning, some would release a cloud of smoke that came straight from their mouths after exhaling their cigarettes. And some..would just make out at random spots in the house, which was starting to make Jo gag at the sight of it.

The whole atmosphere was making him disgusted at the things these teens don't see. They don't see themselves basically wasting their own lives for things so stupid as this. But Axel had to get it through his head that in some way, he was like one of them. Not in the way where he went to parties every weekend, but in the way where life was being wasted every day.

They're all born to die some day. So, therefore, they are all dying slowly. Every day you live would be another day that you're -- in a way -- dying on. Of course, he didn't realize it 'til now that in all the days that he lived in, he was slowly living closer to his death. And that's how life seemed to be -- living as well as dying.

"There!" Jo exclaimed over the music, pointing at the dining room. Standing in the corner of the room was a dark figure with wings attached and a hood over his face. They finally found a demon. The demonic figure was staring hard at two guys who were going at it with each other -- yelling and pointing fingers and shoving each other. He was trying to start a fight.

"You go around the kitchen and I'll take this side," she said, already on the verge of walking towards the dining room.

"Jo," he called, taking a soft grip of her arm. She turned to face him. "Just be careful, okay?"

She nodded and he let her go as he hurried through the kitchen, finding the other doorway that led into the dining room. Peeking through the hallway, he saw how focused the demon was on making the two guys continue the fight he had just started. You could barely tell what his face looked like. You could see his eyes and parts of the face, but no details. Axel thought fast and leaned against the door frame -- with his wings hidden on the kitchen side of the wall -- and started cheering the fight on as if he was a part of the living.

From the other side, he quickly glanced at Jo's confused expression but then she understood what he was trying to do. So she did the same -- except she was pretending to check Axel Lardica out the way girls do when they see a guy. It felt odd glancing at her ever so often with a look that he'd never seen from her before. The look of wanting someone to look at her and notice that she's there. It scared him, but he didn't show it. The demon didn't even notice the two, he was still focused on the drunken fight that was getting bigger and bigger. Axel knew that once this fight blew up, the demon would leave and go back to...

That was it. The two guys staggeringly and clumsily were now throwing punches at each other and tackling each other forcefully. The demon smiled as if he was proud of the job he did and walked out of the dining room, passing Axel only by a few inches and headed out the door. Thankfully, the demon's back was facing Axel and therefore didn't even notice Axel's own wings. He signaled Jo to go to the front as he hurried to follow the demon before he lost him.

Rushing out the door, he immediately spotted the demon standing at the center of the street next to a black hole where he quickly jumped in. Jo an Axel raced to it, hoping they wouldn't lose their chance again.

"AXEL!" Jo cried. "I'M SCARED OF HEIGHTS!"

He took her hand in his as they stopped at the edge of the portal. He pulled her body close and wrapped his arms around her waist and enclosed wings. He had his back to the portal so she wouldn't be first going in. "It's okay, I got you. You ready?"

"For Ozias," she responded, keeping her eyes closed and her head against his chest, doing her best not to look down at what may come at them.

Axel leaned far back and they fell into the blackness of Hell, hoping to find the angel among the darkness.

***

"Jo," Axel called.

"Yes?" she said, petrified. She was afraid to open her eyes, thinking they were still in the air.

"We're on the ground," he replied softly. Her eyes slowly opened and she saw that he was right. But she kinda wished she had never opened her eyes.

Looking around they could already tell they were right at the heart of Hell. The ground wasn't made of dirt but more of ash and dust along with the dark stained stuff that everyone from Hell seemed to have on them. Out beyond them was a field of people who were begging and pleading for something as they were getting eaten alive by.... worms?

There were millions of them getting eaten up by billions of slimy worms and were pleading for a drop of water, or an actual light from somewhere, or even E.J. himself. But it was a scary thing to realize that these people were dead souls and they were in Hell, getting their flesh devoured every day by worms and burning up in this hot area. It made her realize that she and Axel were supposed to be here. If Ozias hadn't saved them, this was the afterlife they were to have forever.

She looked out and found that the only light source there was red and it was coming from a grand castle that stood tall among all of this. "Ozias is probably there," she said, pointing at the great building.

"I hope he's not here," Axel mumbled, looking out into the fields of souls.

"Me too," she said, already walking towards the castle with Axel trailing behind.

They might've been about halfway there when they heard the familiar screeching sounds from afar. Whenever they heard that sound, nothing good ever came from it. So in instinct, the two winged mortals ran. And with prediction, flying demons found a new prey to play with. It felt like they were still on the highway trying to find a way to get to her house. Except the two were in demon territory and the situation was a lot worse.

"Now what?" Jo huffed. But Axel couldn't answer because right then, a demon dove and slammed right into him, making them both tumble. It also happened to Jo as a force from above pushed her into the ground of ashes and dust. She managed to push the demon off of her and rolled on all fours until another shoved her to the ground and kept her there with no way of getting back up. Axel was in the same position with his face looking at hers.

"Well, well," one demon said slowly. "We found our catch of the day." The other demons laughed as they grabbed both of their wings and held their hands behind them firmly. Jo's hair was partially in her face, but there was no way to move it back.

"Ahh, lookie here," said the demon that made the earlier comment as he walked up to Jo. "We got a pretty face," he mocked as he gently brushed his fingers against Jo's face and pulled back her hair behind her ear.

"YOU LEAVE HER ALONE!" Axel snarled, as he lunged at the demon but didn't make it far, thanks to his captors who held him back.

"Protective much?" the demon teased him. "I think Abaddon will enjoy having a nice chat with you two."

"Abaddon?" Jo asked, confused. "Why would Abaddon be here?"

"Oh, darling," came the demon as the other demons started chaining them the way Ozias had been chained before. "Abaddon is the King of Hell."

Chapter XIII

Angels Have Fallen

With chains binding them from any chance of escape, Jo and Axel were led into the great castle they had spotted before they were captured by the demons that now had them. Just with a glance inside the place, Jo's body was trembling so hard her chains rattled. Axel every once in awhile would try to maneuver his way towards her for comfort, but the demons had kept the two at a distance.

Finally, they reached the end of the hallway where right in front of them stood tall double doors guarded by a pair of demons who didn't hold any spears or weapons. Their appearance was probably their weapon keeping any one unwanted out from the throne. Then another demon appeared in the picture and went up to the demon leader that brought Jo and Axel. She recognized Dezmon's face as he got closer.

"What do you have here?" Dezmon asked as if he didn't already know the reason for their arrival. He didn't even speak to the two mortals, which made Jo wonder if they had already missed something.

"We found them in the field heading over here and thought we'd give them a big welcome and have Abaddon greet them first," the demon said cheerfully as if this *wasn't* Hell.

Dezmon met both Jo and Axel's eyes before he spoke again. "I'll take them from here," he said, without a smirk or a remark as he stuck his hand out for the chain lines. He didn't look like the Dezmon they had seen before. He wasn't diabolical or taunting or even demonic in any way. He -- right then and there -- looked almost human and not like a beast. All Jo could see on his face was.... regret? Guilt? Something that was keeping him from speaking to them.

"Who are you to tell me to give you *my* rightful prizes?" the demon snapped.

"Says the Second-in-Command," Dezmon replied flatly.

The demon looked in shock as he apologized to Dezmon for the inconvenience and the argument as he handed him the chain links that were attached to Jo and Axel. Dezmon told them to leave the hallway and all the other demons obeyed him. All that was left in the hallway was Dezmon, Jo, and Axel along with an unknown void they had among them.

"What?" Dezmon asked when he realized that Jo had been staring at him for a while.

"No sarcasm? No taunting phrase? Nothing?" she asked him. "Why?"

He didn't reply, which revealed more of those other emotions she had never seen in him.

"Something happened," Axel said, "Didn't it?"

The demon left them in silence again.

"Where's Ozias?" Jo asked.

The demon became tense when she mentioned the angel's name.

"Dezmon," she called again. But instead of answering, he led them towards the huge double doors and pushed one door open so they could get through. On the other side of the door were enormous pillars that stood on both the left and the right of the room parallel from each other. In the back of the room right in the center was a throne bigger that any chair Jo had ever seen. On it was a man who had gray skin and a bald scarred head. He had wings just as dark as all the other demons and wore black as well. But he seemed a few years older and looked to be in charge. Could this be the king that was before them?

Standing next to him in chains wrapped around their necks were two people -- humans perhaps -- who wore black jumpsuits. They both were a few years older as well and had nice brown hair and neutral skin -- one male, and one female. They stared back at Jo and Axel in regret for some....

"Jo," Axel gasped, staring at one of the pillars closest to the throne that stood on the right side. There were demons there trying to scrub something off of that whole section next to that one pillar.

When they got closer to it, Jo realized it was blood that was stained on both the floor and the pillar. Dezmon lowered his head even more as they passed by it -- trying his best not to look at the area the other demons were trying to clean.

Dezmon stopped and bowed to the man on the throne and didn't get up until he was told to. "Some demons found them out in the field heading over here," Dezmon said.

The king looked at the two almost pleased when he spoke, "Are these the two mortals the angel had kept from us?"

Hearing that the king mentioned Ozias brought her to wonder what they had done to him. Where was he? Wouldn't he be chained up with the male and female that stood next to the king as if they were a part of a freak show?

"Yes, Abaddon," Dezmon replied. Jo then got chills that ran down her back.

This was Abaddon? This man probably was the evilest being there was in the afterlife who she had thought up in her head? She didn't exactly picture him that way at all. She could find some features she went by for him but something had happened that made him turn this way -- that made him turn dark.

"Speak your names," Abaddon commanded to the two mortals.

"Jo Silver,"

"Axel Lardica,"

"How did you both die?" the king asked.

"He shot me,"

"Then I shot myself."

The king looked at them. Then he looked at the two unknown humans next to him, then back at Jo and Axel. "Do you know why you're here?"

"No," Axel said quickly before Jo made a remark.

"You're here," the king started, "because you're going to do the same thing that they --," he pointed at both the male and female, "-- did tomorrow on the Sabbath."

Jo and Axel looked at each other in confusion. "Tomorrow?"

Axel asked.

"It has to be done tomorrow," the king replied. "You both have to do it tomorrow before noon," as he turned to Dezmon, "Take them to their chamber."

"Wait," Jo spoke suddenly. "Where's Ozias?"

The king looked at her and chuckled. "You are asking the wrong person that question," the king told her. "Why don't you ask my new Second-in-Command?" Abaddon pointed at Dezmon, who didn't dare look at her or Axel. She waited for an answer but the demon did as he was told and led the two mortals out of the throne room, going into the dark hallways until they made it to one hallway that had metal bars for cell doors. It was quiet, which made the place more terrifying since there was barely any light shining except for in the hallway.

The demon opened one cell door with a key that was similar to the one that was displayed on the mirror in Jo's shed and then took them inside -- latching the long chain line to the wall. Dezmon closed the door behind him and that's when Jo saw it.

Dezmon's hands were stained... with dried blood.

With not much thought to it, Jo gently took a hold of his hands as he was locking the cell door. Surprisingly, he let her though he was tense about having her skin on his. She examined the dried blood that seemed to be partially still wet, which stained her hands as well. This was only a few moments ago.

She looked at the demon, trying not to jump to conclusions but still thinking about what could've happened in all the time they had spent trying to get there. "Dezmon."

"Yeah?" he replied, fearfully.

"Tell me the truth," she begged, trying her best not to break down. "Is this Ozias' blood?"

The demon, who looked to be just a boy looked down at his feet, not saying anything.

"Was Ozias' blood-stained in that throne room?" she asked.

Jo lost grip of the dark boy's hands as he cried out in despair and banged himself against the metal bars of their cell like a mad animal. She told him to stop but he wouldn't so when she had the chance, her hands went through the bars and took ahold of his face and he stopped. His body was trembling and he was breathing violently.

"Please," she begged again, tears streaming down her face.

He opened his mouth but nothing came out except a single tear that streamed down his pale face. But instead of answering Jo, he backed away from her hold and walked away. She begged him to come back, begged him to say what happened, but he didn't stop walking.

Knowing that something happened to the angel made Jo fall into Axel's arms and she sobbed, even more, that night.

Dezmon probably killed Ozias and didn't have the guts to even tell them. All she really could think about was what kind of demon would ever soften up for an angel like Ozias?

***

It was hard to tell the time but it might've been an hour later when Axel heard footsteps coming down the hallway towards their cell. He nudged Jo -- who was curled up in his arms with dried tears in her eyes -- to stay alert.

He was shocked to find Dezmon coming back, carrying a giant figure in his arms. Stopping right at their cell, Axel saw that it was a person he was carrying. The person was wrapped up in a dark blanket, revealing only the head and the bare feet of the person. He immediately recognized the person the demon brought and so did Jo.

"Oh my gosh!" exclaimed Jo as she ran up to the bars. Dezmon set Ozias down on the ground as he grabbed the angel's white converse and shoved them through the bars. He pulled out the same keys from earlier and opened the cell door. Putting Ozias back in his arms he brought him into the cell with the mortals.

"You came back," Axel said to him in awe. "Why?"

Dezmon gently set Ozias down on the ground with the blanket still wrapped around him. Ozias was awake but he wasn't fully comprehending what was going on. It was as if he was drugged or had been given something so he wouldn't feel much.

The demon looked at the two, still giving them a regretful look. "Because I promised him that he will fly again."

Axel looked at Jo, who looked like she almost understood what he meant. Dezmon uncovered the blanket that was over Ozias in order to show what the demon was really talking about. Ozias was still wearing his white pants but his skin was bare and full of dried blood. Right on his back underneath his shoulder blades were two deep slices that had recently been sewn together in the same place his wings should've been. The stitches were rather crooked and uneven but it was closing the two open wounds. Axel couldn't believe that Ozias' wings were gone. Jo started to cry again, gently smoothing Ozias' head for comfort.

"I tried my best but I never learned how to sew," Dezmon said, sounding teary as he looked at the angel who had no wings. "Luckily, I got someone to help fix it."

"Is this what you couldn't tell us?" Jo asked, with her face still puffy. "That you were the one to take his wings from him?"

Dezmon looked too afraid to speak again, so he just nodded instead.

"Why not rub it in our faces?" Axel asked, "Why not just tell us how enjoyable it was to take your enemy's wings from him?"

"Because I didn't enjoy it," the demon protested. "I didn't enjoy any of it. I hated seeing his tears and hearing his painful cry. I knew I shouldn't have done it. I knew it wasn't his fault he pushed me off, it was mine. It was my own fault I went from white to black."

"So why did you do it?" Jo asked.

"I'm a demon," he said flatly, "Demons always have to do the worst things in the world."

"They don't have to," she corrected him.

"But I can never go back," the demon said.

"Go back where?"

"To Heaven," he replied. "I can never see the light anymore."

It became quiet for a while until finally, the demon rose to his feet. "I never was here," he told them as he closed the cell door and locked it.

"Daniel," Axel called, surprised that the demon's real name suited him better than Dezmon. The demon stopped but didn't turn to face them again.

"Yeah?"

"What is Abaddon going to make us do?" he asked him, knowing that he was talking to a person now.

The demon sighed heavily before he spoke. "When Ozias is better, ask him about Genesis." The demon started to walk away again.

"Daniel?" Jo called to him.

The demon stopped again. "Yes?" he said in a whisper.

"Thank you," she told him.

He said nothing but Axel figured his smile was small as he walked away from them.

Axel and Jo agreed to rotate throughout the night. One rested while the other made sure that the wingless angel was okay. They kept Ozias wrapped up in the blanket that Dezmon brought him in with so that he'd be almost as warm as when he wrapped his wings around himself at night. The night felt long as it was the third time Axel was the lookout while Jo slept right next to him. Ozias stirred more than before and moaned every so often. It was during the middle of Axel's watch that Ozias fully came back from whatever it was that had drugged him. He winced out loud in pain as he attempted to get up. Axel stopped him from hurting himself anymore and told him to stay still. Jo woke up and seemed relieved that Ozias was awake.

The boy who had worn all white found their faces and sighed. "What did I tell you two?" he croaked.

"We weren't going to let you go that easily," Jo stated.

"You're stuck with us," Axel added.

"Well, how thoughtful of you," he said flatly, "But that was stupid." He tried getting up again but pain shot through his back and he cried out. Axel reached for him and brought him back to the floor. Ozias uncovered the blanket off of his body and reached behind him, feeling the stitches that were replacing his beautiful, white wings he once had. His face turned to sorrow after realizing there were no wings where they were supposed to be.

"Ozias?" called Jo when the angel's face didn't change.

"They're gone," he said in a void. "They're really gone."

"Ozias," she said, already starting to sob again. "I'm sorry for not listening to you. I should've listened to you and now we got you into this mess. It was our fault as mortals and you were right about..." Ozias didn't look like he was listening to her for he fell into a daze that no one could get him out of. It wasn't that he was trying to ignore her, it was because it was starting to sink in that he no longer had wings. And if he no longer had wings, he was no longer an angel.

So as Jo tried to apologize for everything she had done, Ozias buried his face in his arms on the floor and cried. Axel couldn't hold back his own tears as he watched the angel who was always the strong one out of the three, now shattering into pieces for one of the most important things he had ever owned. Jo placed herself on him, trying to hug him from the ground as Axel did the same. They both knew that they should do more for him after what he had just gone through. But for now, a hug would have to do.

***

It was probably early in the morning when they all woke up from the same position they were in last night. Jo and Axel helped Ozias sit up as they wrapped the blanket around him. His face was as puffy as theirs from the bursting sobs from the night before. He looked down on the ground where his white Converse lay next to his bare feet.

Jo sat on the angel's left side, leaning her body into his and looking at the white Converse as well. Axel sat next to her left side, leaning his back on the wall and stared at the same thing. "I'm sorry," she said for the trillionth time.

"It's okay," Ozias said weakly.

"It doesn't feel okay."

"I know," he agreed, "but don't beat yourself up about it."

"Are you mad at Dezmon?" Axel questioned.

"No."

"It's okay to be mad at him," Jo said softly. "I don't think you have to keep being perfect for us. We get it."

"I can't be mad at him," Ozias said, "I knew it wasn't him that did it."

"But he told us that it was," Axel said confused.

"Who forced him into it?" the wingless angel asked. "Abaddon. I knew he was fighting it, trying to find the light in this. But darkness clouded his own mind. Abaddon's darkness."

"Just like Dezmon did to me?" Axel asked.

"Exactly," Ozias agreed. "Even though I was out of it before, I was pretty shocked when he came for me. Stitched me up with a friend and brought me to you guys. He's willing to change but Abaddon's holding him back."

"Abaddon mentioned to us that we have to do something today," Jo said, recalling the conversation. "We asked Dezmon about it but he told us to ask you about Genesis."

Ozias looked at the two confused, "Genesis?"

"Yeah," she replied. "Abaddon was talking about how we're going to do the same thing that his two human prisoners did before noon today."

"Two human prisoners?"

"They were the two that were next to him on his throne," Axel explained.

"But they are..... oh no!" Ozias said in horror.

"What's wrong?" Jo asked worriedly.

"No no no no no no no. This can't be, it can't be. It's Easter. Today's Easter *Sunday!*"

"Of course it is," Jo said, "it comes every year on a Sunday sometime in the spring. What else is new?"

"Ozias! What are you talking about?" Axel asked, freaking out.

He looked at the two mortals in horror. "This isn't good. I knew you two shouldn't be here and now I know why." He stopped and took a long breath. "Please tell me you know about the story of Adam and Eve?"

"Adam and Eve?" Jo asked, trying to remember the Bible stories from Sunday School when she was younger. "Are they the ones in the garden of Eden that ate some forbidden fruit God told them not to eat and got cast off?"

"Sure, let's go with that," Ozias began. "Adam and Eve were the first people to ever have a close relationship with God, right? Until they ate the fruit from the Tree of Knowledge of Good and Evil and were separated forever from Him, making everyone after them have the curse to be separated from God for thousands of years. That is until finally, E.J. came and sacrificed Himself so that the curse could be broken...."

"Wait, wait, wait," Jo said, "You're telling me that E.J. sacrificed Himself so that the curse could be broken? Isn't that what.... ohhhhh, please tell me I'm not mistaken but isn't that..."

"Uhh, yes it is," Ozias said as if she was supposed to know that. "E.J. stands for Emmanuel Jesus, but everyone around Heaven gave him that nickname -- or mostly the generation that died after the 2000s."

"This is insane," Jo said, not even sure what to believe. "I made a character that's supposed to be *Jesus?*"

"Can we get to the point where everything makes sense?" Axel pointed out.

"As I was saying," Ozias continued, "Abaddon -- who is also known as Satan to all the mortals -- for thousands of years more tried to bring the curse back. And I think he found a way. Those two humans he had, they're Adam and Eve themselves. They went missing for a while after their deaths and now I know where they've been."

"WHAT?" the two mortals exclaimed.

"And since you two are mortals just like them and are descendants of them, Abaddon wants you two to eat the forbidden fruit and recreate the curse," Ozias said, more scared than ever. "On Easter Sunday."

"The day of the resurrection of E.J.," Jo said flatly.

Suddenly, multiple footsteps marched down the hallway towards them. They could hear the snickering and the mockery of demon voices as they got closer to their cell. Dezmon was among them but not as demonic as the others were. "Ready for the big day?" he asked the two mortals unenthusiastically.

"Where are we going?" Jo asked nervously as Dezmon opened the cell door for the other demons to go in and take a hold of both Jo and Axel. Unlatching the chains from the wall, they were shoving them out of the cell as Ozias tried his best to stop them but couldn't.

"We're taking you two to get ready," he said, looking into her eyes as if she needed to pay attention to what he was saying. Like a way of playing it cool before they lost eye contact and were fully out of the cell.

Dragging his way to the cell door as it closed on him, Ozias held onto the bars in order to sit up straight. "Axel, Jo," he called, not even caring that the demons would hear. "Don't do it. No matter what, do not, please do not, do it. I don't care if they hurt me even more, don't do it. *Please!*"

The demons laughed as if it was funny what Ozias was warning them about. One of them put his foot through the metal bars and kicked Ozias right in the face. He cried out in pain as the demons chuckled.

"LEAVE HIM ALONE!!" Jo begged, trying to push past the demons to see if Ozias was okay. Axel did the same but neither of them were able to win over the demonic beasts.

"Enjoy being on the ground," one demon said as they pushed, shoved and dragged Jo and Axel away from the cell. Both mortals tried to fight back but were outnumbered. Seeing Ozias already in pain made Jo feel much worse. She knew she should listen to him and not do it—not eat the fruit but she was tired of bringing Ozias more pain.

She saw how he begged them not to eat the fruit but if she were to continue hurting him, she would have to eat the fruit just like Adam and Eve did.

Even if it meant bringing back the curse on an Easter Sunday.

Chapter XIV

The Sinful Fruit

They were brought out of the cells and into the nicer area of the dark castle with Dezmon in the lead and the demons trailing behind with their prey.

Axel had done his best to stay close to Jo but the demons wouldn't let him. He was worried not just about what they'd do to them but also what they'd do to Ozias. Never in his life had he ever wished so much that he could go back to Texas again and start this whole thing over with them still alive, not prisoners of Hell about to recreate the curse that was now broken.

If E.J. was really the Son of God, then where was he? Did he really not know they were here in the hands of Abaddon? Is he just watching from somewhere deciding to let this happen? To let Axel and Jo pay their price?

His thoughts went to their reality as the demons stopped him in front of a door as the demons holding Jo continued walking ahead.

"AXEL!" she screamed after realizing they were going to split the two mortals up.

"JO! IT'S OKAY!" he assured her. "IT'S OKAY! YOU'RE GOING TO BE FINE!"

"AXEL!" she screamed again, trying to reach to him. One demon picked her up from her waist and continued to take her in the opposite direction. "AXEL!" she cried, kicking and screaming like a young girl as her parents dragged her away.

"It's okay," he said softly as the demons shoved him through the door, not seeing a glimpse more of Jo Silver. He was only able to hear her cries as they started to slowly fade away.

The school shooter was shoved into what looked like a dressing room. There was a section where it was blocked by a long curtain, indicating it was where you change clothes. Covering the walls from floor to ceiling were mirrors all reflecting on him as he stood in the middle while the demons unhooked the chains from him. As they walked out the door, the demonic beasts were toying with him and laughing at him until only Dezmon was left in the room. The boy looked at the demon, hoping for some explanation to this but he didn't give any.

"Is Jo somewhere safe?" he asked the demon.

"Something like it," Dezmon replied. "Do you know if she's going to do it?"

"I don't know," was all he could think to say. It was hard to tell at this point if she was going to fight it off or just eat the sinful fruit and let the curse happen. Would she really do it? Would she do it if it depended on.... "She probably will if they bring Ozias into this," he answered, knowing that it could've been a risk to tell him that but it didn't seem too dangerous to share what the demons probably already knew about.

"Abaddon is planning on it," Dezmon confirmed as he went to the door.

"Daniel," Axel called, hoping that it wasn't a risk there. The demon stopped and waited. "Who's side are you on?"

"Your clothes are on the rack," the demon responded, on the verge of closing the door on him until Axel stopped him before the door became fully closed.

"Who's side are you on?" he asked the demon again.

The demon looked at him as if he was trying to decide right then and there his answer.

"Do you honestly not know?"

"Of course I do," he said quickly. "My colors show what team I'm on." and Dezmon slammed the door on Axel -- leaving the mortal alone in a room with mirrors staring at him as if they knew he was the one who shot Jo Silver in the first place.

***

Jo was done getting dressed in the black jumpsuit that both she and probably Axel were forced into wearing for whatever it was that was coming next. There were two gaps opened in the back of the suit where her wings branched out.

Her long brunette hair was loose, hanging down behind her as she re-tied the bandana on her arm so it wasn't tight inside the sleeves of the suit. She crouched down and shoved her feet into her red shoes again as she thought about what she was being prepared for.

Jo was supposed to eat the sinful fruit that Adam and Eve ate back in the beginning in order to bring the curse back and make Abaddon happy. She wondered if the millions and millions of souls that were out in the field would agree to this. If Jo was out there, knowing more people would suffer as much as she was, then why would she agree to this?

Because maybe she was forced to agree to it, right? They're physically going to force her into eating the fruit and there was nothing she could do about it. But then again, she was lying to herself because Adam and Eve had a choice not to...even though they did. And Jo planned on not eating it, but what if instead of making her do it, they gave her a choice.

What if the choice was saving the world and all the generations after it, or try saving Ozias from any more upcoming pain. That's what it really came down to at this point. Should she not do it and save her family and Avy from suffering like this? Or should she be willing to eat it and save only Ozias who had saved them countless of times?

The door was opened and in came Dezmon himself. He didn't bring anything to tie her with or drag her down with which seemed strange. "It's time," he told her.

"No chains?" she asked, trying to stay on guard.

"Just follow me," he told her, "You'll know why soon enough."

The demon opened the door and walked out as the mortal followed him. That was when she knew why she didn't come out in chains. There were demons against the walls of the hallway, screaming, cheering, mocking, and snickering at her. And there was no end to the demons that watched her as she followed Dezmon closely down the middle to the next place. Even if she did try to run, about thirty of these demons could pounce on her in the blink of an eye.

It felt like they walked through the entire castle when finally Dezmon stopped at another set of double doors that were new to her. Axel stood there wearing the same jumpsuit she had on with his demon guard and she ran up and hugged him tightly.

"Axel."

"It's okay."

"I'm scared," she whispered in his ear. "I don't want to do this."

"Then don't do it," he said simply.

"What about Ozias?" she asked, "What are they going to do to him?"

"He told us to not do it," he told her. "We have to listen to him this time."

"I can't see him hurt anymore," she cried before they were pulled apart.

"That's enough!" snarled the demon that had escorted Axel.

"I'll take it from here," Dezmon told him, and the demon nodded in approval before he left them. Dezmon looked at the two with concern and pity as the demons still roared from where they were.

"You ready?" he asked them.

"For prom or graduation, yes," Jo quipped, "For this, how can you be ready for this?"

It was pretty interesting to see a real smile come from the demon before he turned around and opened the doors and they went through. Inside was a huge room with a concert full of demons screeching and cheering as they laid eyes on the three that had just entered. Jo's adrenaline was pumping as she walked forward behind Dezmon towards the stage that had a giant dark tree there with a single fruit growing on it.

It was the Tree of Knowledge of Good and Evil. Chained to the tree by their ankles were Adam and Eve themselves, staring at both Jo and Axel in sorrow. Abaddon stood there with beaten up Ozias in chains next to him. The wingless angel looked at them with a warning on his face, indicating to remember what he told them before. They stepped on the stage and faced the audience, who were acting like mad animals in the presence of the two mortals. Holding up his hand, Abaddon was able to silence them.

"I believe we all know why we have been gathered here today on this Easter morning," Abaddon said to the crowd. They all cheered for a good few seconds then were silenced again for the King of Hell to continue. "And today is the day we take back what is ours once and for all eternity!" The crowd roared again as Axel took Jo's hand for comfort, watching thousands of demons that wanted them to each take just one bite.

"And to make sure we get what we want, we have our own wingless angel to play with," the king said, referring to Ozias. "Who wants his blood?" he shouted. The crowd was drooling for Ozias as they tried to reach for him, fighting to get closer and closer -- making the king's point for Jo and Axel to see.

How could they do this to them? They were just kids that had died this past week and now these evil spirits had made them into a piece of their plan they never signed up for. And they were willing to tear an innocent wingless angel, limb from limb, to make sure the winged mortals would do exactly what they wanted. All the while Jo watched Dezmon wondering what side he was on in all of this? Ever since he'd cut off Ozias' wings, something in him changed but they weren't even sure where his head was at. He helped Ozias, he brought Jo and Axel into this, he warned them, he obeyed Abaddon. There was no telling who he would fight along with at this point.

"Let us finish what we started!" roared the King of Hell, encouraging the crowd to screech and cheer for this awful ceremony.

Is anyone seeing this? She thought, *Can anyone save us from this wickedness?*

Anyone.

Jo saw Abaddon tell Eve to grab the fruit from the dark tree. Reluctantly, the woman reached for the one and only fruit and picked it off the branch. For a while, she stared at it in her hands and it seemed as though she wasn't going to let it go, but she passed it to Adam.

Someone save us from this. Jo prayed on the inside, *Don't let this happen.*

Adam turned to face Jo, holding the sinful fruit out to her.

Jo heard Ozias begging her not to do it as she picked the fruit up in her hands. The demons that were on the stage were shoving the boy in white closer into the sea of demons that were wanting a hold of the wingless angel.

Save him or save the world.

Jo had to save him.

But what about the world?

Jo brought the fruit closer to her face, hearing Ozias yell even louder at her. He didn't care how loud he'd have to get, he didn't want them to do it. But she had to, right?

Anyone there? She asked one more time, bringing the fruit even closer to her face. *Can anyone hear me?*

Jo Silver opened her mouth as the fruit got closer and then....

It was gone.

Jo was about to take a bite and she realized that Dezmon had snatched it out of her hands. She looked at him in shock. Abaddon's voice paniced as he tried to snap Dezmon out of it. Dezmon held the fruit close to his face as his eyes roamed everywhere -- backing away from Abaddon and closer to Jo and Axel. Gasps filled the audience as they saw what had just happened. Even Adam and Eve's faces had changed into utter shock.

"Daniel?" Ozias called, surprised to find himself calling the demon by his true name.

"I'm tired of being in the dark," was all the demon said right before he took a bite of the sinful fruit. From Dezmon's body shined the brightest light there ever was in Hell which brought every demon and even the king to their knees as they tried to cover their eyes. Dezmon cried out in agony, falling to the ground as he started to change from black to white. A whirl wind blew through the place so hard, Jo struggled to remain standing. The demons ran out the door trying to get away from the bright light as it burned their flesh. Even Abaddon tried to run from the light but it was hard for him since he was one closest to the source. Axel shielded Jo from the wind as they watched Ozias crawl his way to the demon that was hurting the most.

Dezmon screamed and screamed in pain as he finally became white. His hair was still dark as the night and his skin was the same, but his clothes had changed into scattered black and white patches that matched the same pattern on his wings. They were able to find some sections of his wings as white as Ozias'.

The whirling wind was slowly calming down when Dezmon fell

to the floor of the stage. Ozias was able to reach him along with Jo and Axel as they realized that Dezmon was slowly disappearing into smoke and dissolving in the wind.

"Are you crazy?" Ozias told him as he took Dezmon's hand into his with tears streaming down his face. "Why did you do it?"

"What's going on?" Jo cried as she saw Dezmon's feet vanishing.

"I found the light back home, Ozias," Daniel told him as tears streamed down his face. Daniel's knees were starting to dissolve as he pulled out what looked like a necklace. On it were two long feathers were tied together, one was black and the other white. "Here," he said, shoving the necklace into his hands. "Take it."

"Don't you dare do this to me," Ozias said, gripping Daniel's hand tighter than before. Daniel's waist was halfway gone along with his new white wings from the wind by this time. "Don't you dare leave like this."

"Tell my mom goodbye for me," Daniel croaked.

"Ozias! We gotta do something!" Axel cried.

"WE CAN'T!!" Ozias sobbed. "There's nothing we can do about it."

"Ozias," Daniel called softly, as the hand that held Ozias' hand was disappearing.

"Yes?" Ozias replied.

"Go touch the sky for me."

Then before they knew it, the last of Daniel disappeared with the wind.

Ozias clutched the necklace tightly as tears ran down faster than the wind was blowing. Jo thought as she cried that the light within Daniel was gone now until a new light came and shined brighter than the first one. She heard Abaddon screaming in horror as the source of light came closer to them.

Jo Silver tried to detail the figure but all she saw was light before she fell into darkness.

Chapter XV

The Light

Axel gasped for air as he suddenly woke up. He breathed heavily as he realized he was lying in a white bed, with white walls, and wearing white clothes.

He wasn't the only one in the room. Jo was stirring in her sleep on his left side as if she was about to wake up soon. On his right was Ozias who sat up in his bed looking at the necklace Daniel had left him before he disappeared.

"About time you woke up," Ozias said half-jokingly, half focused on the necklace.

"Where are we?" the boy asked him.

"You should take a wild guess," Ozias replied. "I'll give you a hint. If we saw Hell as everything in black, then we are in...."

"Heaven," Jo finished while rubbing her eyes.

"Hey," Axel greeted her.

"Hi," she said, half smiling. She slowly sat up and asked, "How did we get here?"

"I believe he would know," Ozias said, referring to the man who stood at the door. He was tall and a lot older than the other three. His wings were as white as the room with not a speck of black on them. "Hey, Gabe," Ozias said to the angel.

"Ozias," Gabe nodded. "How are you doing?"

"Better than yesterday," Ozias replied. "What's up with you?"

"He wants to see Josephine Silver and Axel Lardica," the angel told them.

"Who does?" Jo asked, confused.

"I believe you already know who," Gabe told them. "Follow me."

They both looked at Ozias for help. "It's okay," he told them, "I'll be here." With instinct, they both got up but instead of following right away, they went to Ozias and embraced him partly because they felt like they needed to and partly because it wouldn't feel right to just walk away.

"You know I'll always be right here with you two," Ozias said.

"We know," Jo said, "But we'll be here for you also."

"Even if you get tired of us mortals, you're just going to be stuck with us for awhile," Axel joked and they all broke into a laugh.

"I'm sorry about Daniel," Jo whispered in the wingless angel's ear.

"Me too," Axel added.

"Seeing him almost as white as he was before made me remember all the good things that were in him," Ozias said, "I'm glad he found the light back home."

"How exactly did he die?" Jo asked as they broke the hug.

The angel sighed. "Immortals -- whether they are angels or demons -- can never eat the fruit from the Tree of Knowledge of Good and Evil because it will kill them if they try. Seeing all that should never be seen along with the light burning in them will cause them to vanish from existence for eternity. Only mortals can take half of that and still live through it."

"So Daniel is gone for good?" Axel asked, "There's no way to bring him back?"

"Yeah," Ozias said in a void, "He's really gone from existence unless God Himself would be kind enough to bring him back."

"Don't let me be gone," Jo whispered to herself.

"What?" Axel asked her.

"Don't let me be gone," Jo repeated louder than the first time. "From Twenty One Pilots' song 'Goner'. Just as Avy said it for us, don't let Daniel be gone from us."

The angel smiled. "Always,"

"And forevermore," Axel finished. After going through that tender moment of remembering Daniel, the two then faced the angel who waited patiently at the door.

And as always, the two mortals followed.

Gabe led them through many hallways making the place into a maze unless, of course, you knew where you were going. Axel lost track at how many turns they made since they left Ozias back in the room they woke up in. Heaven was obviously so much nicer and much more comforting that Hell. Axel was glad he wasn't hearing any souls cry out in pain from the worms eating their flesh.

Instead, he could hear billions, or even trillions of voices singing joyfully and with triumph as one choir, making Axel realize this was the complete opposite of what Hell was like. Gabe stopped at double doors that were wide open. "Go right in," the angel encouraged. "He's really wanting to see you two."

They both thanked the angel and went in. Standing on a balcony area looking out beyond him with his back facing them was a man who looked a similar age to Abaddon and they both quietly went up to him. He had a nicer brown color hair than Jo's and his skin was neutral. Just like everyone else in Heaven, he wore all white. They waited to see if he had noticed the two mortals were present behind him.

Finally, he turned around and faced them with a smile. "Glad you both were able to recover well," he said to them,

"Thank you, uhh, sir," Jo said quickly.

"You can call me E.J. if you like," E.J. told them.

"Okay," she replied nervously.

"Were you the light that came to us?" Axel asked him as he remembered the second light after Daniel's.

"Yes, I was," he replied. "I heard both of your prayers."

"You did?" Jo asked surprisingly.

"Every single word," he said, "Come over here and see this." They both came close to the balcony as they saw what E.J. had been watching for awhile. It was the bright sky above them and the earth below them. They thought they could see every single city there was from there, as its lights shined for all of Heaven to see. It was so beautiful yet difficult to comprehend how it was possible that they could see the entire earth flat at just one glance.

"Isn't it marvelous?" E.J. asked them.

"Indescribable," was all Jo could get out of her mouth.

"Is this how you thought of me for your story?" he asked her. Jo looked at him surprised to hear he knew about that. Axel was shocked as well but maybe E.J. knew about it all along. Of course, he could've, he was the Son of God.

"Well, umm," she started as if she tried to find a way to explain her answer to him. She looked out beyond them, seeing the world below as she spoke. "Not really because none of the four guys I imagined were what I had thought you all would be. And in a way, it is a good thing because I don't think I would've been able to find a story greater than this one."

E.J. nodded as he listened to her. He then turned to Axel. "Have you found your second chance?"

"I believe you already gave me my second chance," Axel replied. "We were in Hell and you came for us. You came for us even though we weren't supposed to be here in Heaven, with you. Ozias did the same thing, even though he broke the rules, he broke them for us."

"I don't get it," Jo said, looking out at the earth below them. "How exactly were we supposed to die and come up here to Heaven? What did we -- what did everyone else burning in Hell -- miss or not have that was supposed to take us here?"

"Well, you both didn't believe and neither did the rest of the people that are in Hell," E.J. told them.

"Believe?" Axel asked, "Believe in what?"

"Believe in me," E.J. replied, "I am the only way to eternal life, you know? All it took was to just believe that I am there for you just as Ozias has been there for Avy. To believe in me is to find the light back home."

That's when Axel realized what Daniel was talking about when he mentioned he found the light back home. He found the light back to E.J. -- the eternal home. Axel wondered if that was really the key to life for the living -- the key to finding their way back home.

"Tell me something, you two," E.J. questioned, "what is it that will stick with you forever from all of this?"

They both looked at each other as if their answer could be read on each other's faces but wasn't. It was interesting to find Axel thinking about this experience that would never drift away from his mind. There were a lot of things he learned but only one would really stick with him forever. Only one thing would always come back to mind ever so often through the rest of eternity.

"For me," he started, thinking carefully on what he was about to say, "It would have to be sacrifices are choices you decide to make for the people you care for. Ozias did it for us, Daniel did it, in the end, we did when we went after Ozias, and you did too. You give up something -- your wings, your life, your journey, your light -- because you want to protect the people you love. And that to me, becomes a true sacrifice."

"That's true," Jo agreed, "because it takes something greater to go deeper and find that story to tell. The story of love, life, death, friendship, light, dark, and sacrifice. There's no way to write a great story if you can't live your story fully without those key things. Which is kinda why," she paused, peering into E.J.'s eyes. "I'm asking you to have my wings removed and be given to Ozias."

E.J. looked stunned but still seemed well aware of the news. "May I ask why?" he asked.

"Because in his story, he made the biggest sacrifice as an angel to have his wings cut off," Jo replied, "And he did it for us -- he went to Hell for us -- knowing he may never be an angel again."

"Daniel said that one day, Ozias will fly again," Axel added, "and I want him to fly with my wings as well."

E.J. looked at them, smiling at the sacrifice they were willing to make for the angel that became their friend. "I believe that is possible. Ozias shall have the left wing of Jo and the right wing of Axel which will represent the Heart and Bravery of both Josephine Silver and Axel Lardica."

"I think Ozias would love that," Jo said smiling.

"You know," E.J. started with a matter-of-fact tone, "He would also love it if you both take your last flight with both of those wings still on your back."

"Oh no, I couldn't," Jo said immediately, "I don't do well with heights."

"C'mon Jo," Axel called, taking her hand. "You can do it. Let's do it for Ozias."

She still looked nervous about it, but then agreed to do it for the angel. One last flight was all that was left for them to do to send these wings up high. E.J. helped the two get up on top of the balcony white stone railing. Axel still held Jo's hand as they stood there for a good few moments of capturing the view from where they were.

"Are you ready?" he asked her.

"Let's touch the sky," she replied.

They both jumped off, falling into what felt like the universe.

Until they found the wind in their wings and touched the sky.

After acknowledging E.J. from the sky, Jo and Axel went closer towards the light until they were suddenly blinded by it, as darkness came upon them suddenly.

Chapter XVI

Endings Become Beginnings

"Pancakes!" hollered her mother from the kitchen that was down the hall from Jo's room. Jo moaned as the sun was shining right at her squinting eyes as she pulled the covers off of her bed...

Jo froze with her eyes wide open as she sat up on her bed.

Her bed.

It was morning and Jo Silver was in *her* room laying in *her* bed when her mother hollered, Pancakes."

Did she really just hear her mother yell about pancakes being ready for breakfast?

No, she couldn't have. This has to be some kind of dream.

She remembered flying and facing her fear of heights in Heaven before she gave up her wings to Ozias. Remembering the angel, Jo reached for her back, searching for her wings that weren't there anymore. Not a trace of a scar from them ever existing underneath her shoulder blades. She must have been in surgery or something so that her wings could be cut off carefully for Ozias to use. There was no way she was alive.

But then again, she didn't remember trying to prepare herself for surgery. So how was this happening right now? How was she here?

"JO!!! ARE YOU UP?" called her mother again, sounding louder than the previous call for pancakes. Quickly, Jo rushed out of her bed and ran straight into the kitchen.

"Mom?"

"Well aren't you gonna get dressed, honey?" she asked as she put some pancakes on a plate. "You're not going to go to school in your pj's are you?" she teased.

"School?" Jo asked. "What's today?"

"Umm, today is Monday Jo," her mother said.

"The Monday after Easter?" Jo asked. "Saturday was my funeral, right?"

Her mother looked at her with one eyebrow up. "Your funeral? Easter? Easter's this upcoming Sunday."

"*Upcoming Sunday?* This has got to be a dream," Jo said to herself. "The wings shouldn't take that long to be removed, right?"

"Wings?" her mother asked her. "Jo, what are you talking about?"

"Nothing," she said, "This is all a dream. I'll wake up from it and I'll see Heaven again."

"Heaven?" her mother asked, sounding worried. "Jo, are you not feeling well or something?" she asked her daughter as she touched Jo's forehead to check her temperature. Feeling her mother's skin on hers was what made her flashback to the things that happened the Monday she was shot by Axel.

Her mother was now wearing the same thing she did that day. She was making the same breakfast she made on that Monday as well. Her skin felt so real on hers.

"Well you feel fine so I don't understand why..." Jo's mother couldn't finish her sentence before her daughter quickly embraced her as she was on the verge of joyful tears saying how much she had missed her. When her father came into the kitchen, it became so much more intense as Jo tried to grasp both of them, hoping she wouldn't wake up from the dream she was in. They both then reminded her about how she was going to be late for school so she rushed back to her room and changed into the same clothes she had worn that Monday--along with the black bandana she wrapped around her wrist.

After getting her stuff and hugging her parent's goodbye with a true heart, she ran to the bus stop where she saw Avy, who was stalling the bus driver so she could make it onto the bus.

"You're late," Avy told her in the same way as that horrible Monday they both got on the bus together.

"Avy? Are you okay?" Jo asked her.

"Yeah," she replied, moving into one of the rows on the bus, saving room for Jo to sit in as well. "But you don't seem okay to me. You look like you played Five Nights At Freddy's all night and couldn't sleep at all because of how scared you get when you play that game. What's wrong?"

"I'm in a dream," Jo told her, "This has to be a dream. Because I saw you when I died and you were at my funeral and you did an eulogy for both Axel and I. And Ozias was really afraid to tell you that you weren't alone because he was your..."

"Woah, Woah, Woah!" Avy said with her hands up. "You're talking nonsense about you being dead, which is obviously not true, and what eulogy? Who are Axel and Ozias?"

"Axel is the guy that shot me," Jo told her as if Avy was supposed to know this already – which she did.

"*Shot* you?" Avy repeated, looking more worried at her best friend. "Alright, what did you watch without me?"

"You don't remember?"

"Remember what?"

"I was dead and I missed your ballet recital because I was shot by Axel. You don't remember?"

"Jo," Avy said, "my recital is this Friday. Are you sure you're okay? 'Cause I'm pretty sure you watched a Walking Dead episode without me and got pretty freaked out."

This dream didn't make sense at all. Jo was confused. Why was she back to this same Monday? Back to this Monday where she had been shot? Where was the angel Ozias? Why wasn't he here in the dream she was in? Maybe Jo had to do something to wake up from it. Maybe the wings are already off of her and she just has to wake up. But how?

"Can I ask you something, Avy?"

"Go for it, girl." her friend replied, nervously. "As long as it's not about you disagreeing that Hawkeye should get his own movie. Now that might end our friendship right there. We've been sending Marvel letters for months about this important issue so I'm not going to let you back down on this."

"This is going to sound weird," Jo started, doing her best to sound serious after laughing about Avy believing that Jo was going to give up on Hawkeye -- who was destined to be her husband one day. "But I want to ask your thoughts about miscarried babies?"

***

"So you don't think they still live on do you?" Jo asked curiously as the two got off of the bus as it stopped right in front of the school.

"Well," Avy started, "how can they if they have never been born in the first place?"

"But what if they do?" Jo urged, "what if they still exist in the afterlife and are watching us right now?"

"I don't know," her best friend told her, "then I guess I have a dead older brother."

"Older brother?" Jo repeated, sounding slightly excited.

"Yeah," Avy replied, "My parents had a miscarriage two years before I was born. It was a boy and they had a name planned out and everything but I can't remember what it was. But his heart stopped then he was gone."

"Oh wow," Jo exclaimed, trying to have sympathy in her voice. "Did they tell you about it?"

"Nah," Avy said, "I found some baby stuff in the attic one day with the letter 'O' on it and asked what it was for. I swear it was a strange name like Oliver or Obediah or something. I think it was about the time I met you."

"Interesting timing," Jo pointed out as they went into the building to start school. All the classes Jo was in were teaching the same thing as the Monday when she was shot. She could recite almost everything that happened during all those classes and what they had taught on that familiar Monday. She kept trying to think about how to wake up from this long dream she was having and get back to Heaven where Ozias and Axel were along with E.J. Jo thought she was supposed to wake up by now but the day went on until finally, lunch came. Jo sat down with Avy, trying to think this through when her best friend spoke.

"Still on that miscarriage thing?" she asked Jo, already reading her face.

"No, I was trying to figure something out."

"I'll go get Cokes for us, then," Avy told her as she got up and left Jo to continue thinking.

There had to be another way out of this. The living could see her and it seemed rather odd at this point. She was so used to being invisible and it felt weird having eyes on her or glancing at her as she went through all of this. So if this was the Monday Axel shot her and it was going exactly how it went then-- with minor differences -- then wouldn't Axel be here as well?

Wait...

Jo was the one who got the Cokes before, not Avy.

Jo jumped out of her seat and rushed to the soda machines where Avy stood, suddenly looking at glitches of a figure next to her with the two Cokes in her hands. Jo stood at a distance as teens passed through her view of Avy. As the teens passed by, Jo could almost catch glimpses of a white figure next to Avy. The figure would appeared on and off every time someone went by and Jo realized this wasn't a random figure next to Avy Whitman.

The figure who had Jo's and Axel's wings on its back, shoulder brushed on Avy's, peered at her with its blue eyes. She could see that their lips moving. She looked amazed and rather shocked at the figure that stood next to her. Jo didn't dare move because she didn't want to interrupt this moment of one Whitman saying hi to the other Whitman. It was something Jo had dreamed of witnessing ever since the three of them went to Avy's recital.

And now, it was finally happening.

The angel said something else and vanished away -- after giving a smile to Jo -- with Avy trying to find him again. Jo then walked up to her as if she saw nothing.

"Did you see *that?*" Avy asked.

"See what?"

"Th-There was a boy here about a few years older than me," Avy started, pointing at the spot that Ozias was before he left. "And he was in all white and had these beautiful wings. He looked so real and I couldn't believe what I was seeing. Please tell me you saw it."

"I don't think I did," Jo told her, "Did this boy say anything to you?"

"Yeah," she replied, "he said hi, then I said hi and then he was gone, Jo! I'm not making this up, you have to believe me, Jo! He was there!"

"Don't worry Avy," Jo assured her, "I believe you..."

"I didn't even get his name or anything but he was there, Jo! I wish I knew who he was," she said.

"Well Avy," Jo called, "Maybe one day you'll know."

***

Jo walked to her house after being dropped off by the bus after school let out. Avy would've joined her at her house to catch up on some Once Upon A Time episodes after both attempted to do schoolwork, but she had an understandable excuse of having dance rehearsal for her recital on Friday night.

She was one of the last people to get off at her stop this was the first time ever she had talked to the bus driver, Mrs. Maine -- Daniel's mother -- about one day during the week or the weekend getting together to talk or have a meal together or some kind of interaction besides just taking her to school every day.

Surprised as she was, Mrs. Maine happily agreed to the idea. The bus driver had no clue as to why the teenager would ask anything of her -- let alone, ask her if she'd be willing to go out together.

Well, at least Jo found a way to get her to meet up because she had been wanting to talk to her about Daniel and who he really was to Mrs. Maine.

It was a sunny spring day in April. The wind was blowing and Jo noticed the trees were blooming as she made her way up the hill to where her house was. She looked down the road at the bottom, remembering the flight lessons Ozias had given both to Axel and herself on this same hill.

It was Friday -- Good Friday to be exact. The same day of Avy's recital. In a way, it was kind of cool taking flight lessons with an angel.

Who really gets to do that? Not many. Though on that day, Jo was struggling to fly due to her fear of heights, and yet, she still had a friend and an angel friend that believed in her.

Smiling, she turned back towards the top of the hill, spotting the large cherry blossom tree that was blooming that day as it always did every spring. Jo stopped and stared at the mailbox that stood right next to the tree, where Axel was waiting for her.

"AXEL!" she screamed as she ran up to him, dropping her backpack on the lawn along the way and jumped on him. He staggered back but didn't fall to the ground, as his arms became tangled around her.

"JO! IT'S REALLY YOU!!" he cried, as his eyes met hers. "I CAN'T BELIEVE WE'RE HERE!" he said as he set her down on her feet and meeting her eyes with his. "Jo, I broke the gun!"

"You what?" she asked, confused.

"I broke the gun," he repeated. "This morning, I woke up back where I was in my truck, parked in the school parking lot with the gun right next to me, loaded and everything. I didn't hear Dezmon trying to manipulate me or anything. So right then and there, I decided to break the gun.

"And I called my mom and told her how sorry I was for leaving her, told her where I was, and that I would be back home soon. I then drove here and waited all day for you to come home because today is the day we live! Today is the day we believe in the things that matter!"

"Axel," she said, stopping him. "That's great but, isn't this just a dream?"

"No," he told her, "It's real, Jo. It's all real! We are living."

"We can't be," Jo argued. "We've been dead for a week and there is no other way that..."

"Jo," he stopped her. "How else do you explain why we came back to today -- on this Monday that started this entire thing." He looked at her with hope in his eyes as she stared back at him in disbelief. His face changed into a frown. "You don't believe me?"

"Yeah, well umm, of course, I do." she hesitated. "But how am I supposed to believe that this is real, Axel? It feels so real, yet I know reality says that we're dead and in Heaven and we're just dreaming..."

"Jo," he said.

"Yeah?"

"Don't you believe that E.J. gave us a second chance at this?" Axel asked her. "A chance for us to believe and find our way back home in this life?"

Jo didn't answer, she couldn't answer because she had no idea what to tell him. She thought it was all still a dream and that they were still dead and in Heaven.

"I know I broke the promise the first time around and I won't let that happen again," Axel started, "but you also promised me something too, remember?"

"Yes, I remember," Jo replied. "But.."

"Are you going to do it?" he asked her. "Are you going to keep your promise and write their stories with ours? Because I am here with a second chance and I plan to not mess it up this time. What about you? Do you still think this is all a dream? Because I don't. I think this is real and I usually know what's real and what's not."

Jo looked at him, knowing that deep down inside, Axel Lardica was right. How could this be a dream when they landed right back where the whole thing started? It couldn't have been a coincidence. Just as she remembered Ozias said, probably more than once— everything happens for a reason.

So they were given a second chance on this Monday. Except for this time around, they made it better somehow. Jo woke up with a story. Ozias finally touched Avy and let her feel his presence. Axel broke the gun that shot through the things he had cared about before. And it was all because they had been given a second chance.

So Axel Lardica was right. Jo Silver was truly alive!

"Yes," she told him, "I'm going to write it. I'm going to write the story." She hugged him again, knowing for sure that this time, it was all real.

"I'll have to read this epic story one day," he whispered in her ear, making Jo smile.

"I think you'll be more involved in the writing process than any-one else." she joked. "But more importantly, I'm going to make sure I won't forget any of this. That I remember the reason why you came back, the selfless angel and crazy demon we met— And to remind myself to believe in the people I need to believe in."

"I'm going to believe in E.J.'s second chance," Axel agreed. "There is nothing greater than Him giving us this chance to live again."

Just then a gust of spring wind blew through their hair and blew loose pedals from the blossom tree forming into something unusual. Axel and Jo immediately saw two silhouettes formed by flower petals being carried by the wind towards the sky. They looked like two people with wings -- angels to be exact -- flying above the two mortals with quick glitches of figures looking just as real as the two friends. They both recognized one of them to be the one and only Ozias Whitman as he flew closer to them. The other silhouette seemed rather familiar but the details showed a different person, a new person they all thought they would never see again.

A boy with wings who found his way back home to the light again.

"Daniel was right about one thing," Jo said as Ozias and Daniel's hidden figures went up in the sky leaving their sight getting closer to the sun high above them.

"What was he right about?" Axel asked, looking at her.

"That one day, Ozias would fly again," Jo said, looking back at him, smiling. "And today, he did."

Author's Note

I'm glad you've made it to the end of the book and decided to read this Author's Note. I have added this in order to explain some of the questions you, the reader, may have about The Afterlife Mortals.

The Afterlife Mortals was a story that no matter how much I tried to ignore or shove to the back-burner, it always came back to my mind. I never really knew the end until probably right after I started writing the last chapter. In fact, I barely knew the entire story until I was writing it in the moment.

This story was based mostly on all the school shootings and bombings that have been happening lately in the U.S. -- and even around the world. It has started to become a life and death situation where you can never tell what will happen every time you leave your house. This book represents that we don't have all our days ahead of us written in stone. We only have what was yesterday and right now which is why we have to make it count every time we inhale, exhale, blink, or just think. Carpe diem, seize the day, and so on.

The location I based this story off of was in my hometown in Georgia where I grew up until I moved when I was thirteen. There was no other place I would rather write this story about than in the town I grew up in, which to me will always be home. Some of the things mentioned about this town actually did or still do exist now; such as the ice cream shop, Jo's house on top of a hill (which happened to be the house I grew up in), the school, the civic center where Avy had her recital, and the ceremony for Jo and Axel's funeral.

Jo's personality was partially based off of mine but in some ways, she's based uniquely on herself. Yes, I am the fan girl of anything I can get a hold of—whether it's music, books, or movies. Trust and believe—I will randomly quote any references I've laid eyes and ears on. But I never had a fear of heights although I do have friends who do, which is probably where I got that trait from for the book.

Growing up, after my aunt from Mexico gave me my first pair of black Converse when I was almost ten, my parents had been willing to give me a different pair each year for my birthday or Christmas which is how I brought up the idea of the new Converse each year idea for Jo. The most important pairs of Converse I had was my fifteenth (royal blue) and sixteenth (red) birthdays so far. So you can pretty much guess how old Jo was at the time in the book.

Axel was based mostly off of school shooters that make it on the news—the ones that probably don't understand what they are really doing and are probably just lost. His story of being manipulated by demons or the enemy himself is based on everyone that has gone through something in their life whether it's depression, addiction, or any other struggle there is in the world we live in today.

He's also been based on the amazing friends I grew up with in my hometown and still have to this day. You can never really forget those kind of people—the ones you knew since you were six. These are the friends I could always text or call and it's as if we saw each other yesterday. You know who you are; so thank you!

Ozias is a character that exists in people today. There are some people who are willing to make sacrifices for the people they love most -- even if it means losing their wings. He also represents the miscarried souls that still exist in the afterlife as of now and can't wait to see their parents one day in Heaven. Just like Ozias watches over Avy, so will they for us.

Avy represents the new friends I made after I moved from my hometown. Though there were some hard times I struggled with, these new friends have helped me realize you can always find something new in someone when you are willing to become their friend and get to know them just as if you had grown up with them your whole life. Again, you know who you are; so once again, thanks for your friendships!

Dezmon -- or Daniel -- who was at first known as the antagonist of the story until you realize that deep down inside, he was just a lost boy who couldn't find the light back home until the very end. He represents the aborted babies that didn't have a chance to live. This is just how I pictured one flawed soul having anger towards the mother or even father who decided to let him go. This for me is a way to show that these unborn babies actually matter just as much as we do. Their lives count once they're conceived and we have to remember they are as important as we are when it comes to living and dying. No one deserves to have a chance to live be taken away from them.

The entire book was based on my faith in Christ -- with a mix of my own imagination added to it. The following will explain what's from verses in the Bible and my belief as well as what I made into my own;

Adam and Eve really did exist as the first male and female in the world (Genesis 1:26-27) as they lived in the Garden of Eden until Satan -- or Abaddon in this story -- tricked them into eating the Sinful Fruit (Genesis 3:1-6) and they were cursed by being separated from God (Genesis 3:23). After they were deceased -- or anyone really --, it's hard to know if someone has gone to Heaven or Hell. To me personally, I picture them fallen into Hell or taken by Hell as prisoners since their death just as in the book, but who knows?

Now I believe that E.J. -- who is well-known as Jesus Christ in real life-- and Abaddon --who was Satan and Lucifer before that -- once had a friendship as an angel and as the Son of God until Lucifer became the first fallen angel sent to Hell along with the other angels that followed him (Ezekiel 28:11-19, Isaiah 14). He wanted to be like God and turned wicked, making his wings grow dark, which was the main cause that ended the friendship they probably once had.

Maybe there was something else to the fall of Lucifer, but I guess that's a different story I'll have to one day tell in my own way.

Until then, hope this story will live on with you.

Fill Empty Pages,

-- A.M. Romero

www.ingramcontent.com/pod-product-compliance
Lightning Source LLC
Chambersburg PA
CBHW071402170626
46811CB00003B/1223